Richard Carpenter's

ROBIN OF SHERWOOD

THE SCATHLOCK WOMAN

Richard Carpenter's
Robin of Sherwood
The Scathlock Woman
By Jennifer Ash
Published in 2025 by
Chinbeard Books

in association with
Oak Tree Books
oaktreebooks.uk

Editor: Barnaby Eaton-Jones
Sub Editor: Harriet Whitehouse

Richard Carpenter's

ROBIN OF SHERWOOD

THE SCATHLOCK WOMAN

by
Jennifer Ash

A Chinbeard Books / Oak Tree Books Original

This story is set between
Fitzwarren's Well and
The Time of the Wolf.

PROLOGUE

Elin urged his horse on.

The vibration of the wagon as it bounced over the twigs and tree roots that littered the narrow woodland road added to his anxiety as he peered left, then right, through the trees. This might not have been Sherwood, but he wasn't naïve enough to think that Robin Hood was the only outlaw in England ready to steal from a tax collector.

Steering his horse away from the heart of Cannock Chase and into Pipehall Wood, the final stretch of woodland before he reached Lichfield, the Welshman dared to relax his constant vigil for trouble. Elin fancied he could already taste the ale he'd be drinking once he reached the sheriff's sergeant's office.

Perhaps I'll get a pie too... something warm to—

'Drop your reins!'

Yanking the wagon to a sudden stop, Elin's corpulent frame almost flew over his neighing horse's head in his hurry to do what he was told, as two figures emerged from the trees, their bows drawn.

'Please—don't shoot me!'

'If you don't move, we won't shoot.' A pair of hazel eyes gleamed from beneath a dark brown hood, but Elin didn't notice them. All he saw was the sharp tip of the arrow that was pointing in his direction.

'Alright!' Elin covered his face with his hands. 'Just don't shoo—'

The second assailant turned to the first. 'A coward—what a surprise! Why are tax collectors always such cowards?'

'Because no one with any backbone would do such a terrible job.' The first outlaw circled around to the other side of the wagon, getting closer to Elin in the process. 'Is there anyone in the cart guarding the money?'

'No, no—it's just me.'

'Are you sure?' Firing an arrow that hit the cart just above the taxman's head, the outlaw watched as the tax man squealed in horror.

'Yes, I'm sure! I told you. I work alone!'

'We heard you, you snivelling Welshman.' Making sure their hood was firmly covering their face, the first outlaw came to Elin's side, before waving a hand at their companion. 'Get the money.'

Keeping their weapon aimed at the Welshman's round belly, the first outlaw felt their heart pound with a mix of fear and excitement as they waited; watching as their colleague warily edged to the back of the wagon. 'Let's see how much you've been extorting from the people.'

'I don't extort from anyone! It's my job to collect the king's money—it's his orders I follow!' Dots of perspiration formed on Elin's forehead as he blustered, 'If I don't get this lot to the sheriff, he'll have my ears! Then he'll send me to King John, who'll have me killed!'

Unmoved, his attacker heard the wagon's door being opened. 'The people you took this from could starve! Don't you care that—'

'You liar!' screamed the second outlaw from the rear of the wagon. 'Guards! Inside! Two of them!'

As the armed men leapt from the back of the cart, their swords drawn, the first outlaw snarled as they lowered their bow and grabbed their sword. 'You lying...'

The moment his attacker's attention was off him, Elin gathered up the reins and urged his horse forwards with a crow of laughter.

'Fancy putting down your bow and swapping to a sword! You could have shot all of us! Amateurs!' With a self-satisfied grin he continued to goad his attackers as he rode out of reach. 'Good luck with trying to be second-rate Robin Hoods!'

'Coward!' Yelling after the fleeing wagon, the tax man's mocking words hanging in the air around them, the first outlaw leant their strength to the fight as one of the guards had run forward to take them on. Parry for parry, blow for blow, the first outlaw matched their opponent; what they lacked in experience they more than made up for with sheer will and desperate determination.

They'd just gained the upper hand when a cry of pain told the first outlaw that their accomplice had overcome *their* soldier they were fighting—a cry of pain which was soon followed by the sound of a man crumpling to the ground with some sort of wound.

A second later, from only those few yards away, came the shout from the second outlaw of, 'Your hood!'

Damn! Fira tugged her hood back up. She'd

been so caught up in her swordfight, that she hadn't noticed it had fallen. Cursing, she fought harder.

The sight of the young woman's long red hair held no significance for the man she was fighting— he was too amazed that he was struggling to best a woman in combat to give any immediate thought to the situation, beyond his desire to stay alive. But to Elin, as he rode off in the cart, it meant a good deal.

The Welshman, observing the fight from a safe distance, gave a lazy smile. 'The Scathlock woman! That would explain her temper—and her bravery. Well then… I wonder what the sheriff's man will have to say about that?'

As the cart finally trundled out of view, Fira delivered a knock-out blow to her opponent, and both outlaws—leaving behind their soldier spoils— raced away from the scene too.

CHAPTER ONE

The scratch of the quill as it was laboriously dragged over a piece of parchment was accompanied by a consistent, grumbling commentary.

'Why De Rainault won't pay for a new clerk to come and help me with the tax paperwork, I don't know.' Throwing down the quill in frustration, William Sparrow, the sheriff's sergeant for Lichfield, stared into the fire that dwindled in the grate. 'How is it *my* fault that Elin was robbed by Robin Hood the last two times he took the tax money to Nottingham? It's 'is fault—everyone knows you can't trust a Welshman.'

Picking his quill back up, he dipped it into the murky ink quill. 'I hate it when the sheriff gets cross—he loses all reason; his eyes go all bulgy and—'

The sound of a horse and wagon pulling up outside stopped his grouching in mid-flow. 'Interruptions! That's all I need.' Sparrow rested the quill against the ink well, as heavy footsteps stamped in his direction. 'Now, who's that?'

'Sparrow!' Elin bellowed as he came through the door.

'Oh, it's you.' Sparrow blotted a rogue ink spot that had dripped onto the account list he'd been compiling. 'Welsh charms worked their magic on the people, then? Taxes all collected?'

Elin snorted. 'Collected, yes. Safe, yes. But only just.'

'Only just?'

'I *almost* lost them in Pipehall Wood.'

'Lost them? But you're nowhere near Sherwood, and—'

'I encountered some would-be cutthroats.' Elin stated, folding his arms across his chest. 'My men sorted them out, though. We still have the tax money.'

Jumping up from his stool, Sparrow rested both his palms on his desk, fear creeping up his spine due to the shortening of his own life expectancy. 'Cutthroats? Here, in Lichfield?'

'I said, *would-be* cutthroats.'

Sparrow sprang from his desk, hurrying to peek out through the gap in his shuttered window.

Slumping into a chair, Elin helped himself to some ale from a flagon on the desk. 'Calm yourself, Sparrow; they aren't marching down the streets. There were only two of them anyway.'

'Two or twenty-two is no matter!' Sparrow returned to his stool and thumped a fist onto the desk, almost toppling his goblet of ale. 'The Sheriff of Nottingham will have my hide if he hears about this. He's *always* cross with me…' He trailed off, as if reluctant to go into details about the reason for his employer's latest displeasure.

His curiosity piqued, Elin asked, 'Why would that be?'

'It doesn't matter—but this! Cutthroats near Lichfield? That's a serious matter, and De Rainault will act like it's my fault. He'll make it sound as if *I* invited them here.'

'Indeed he would. But, luckily for you, I know who one of them is. And although they haven't been outlawed yet, it'll only be a matter of time before they are. Unless you catch them, that is.'

Sparrow leant forward eagerly. 'You *know* one of them?'

'Aye, and so do you. A brave and impetus lass, I'll

give her that—clearly no common sense, though. It must run in the family,' Elin's Welsh accent boomed around the confided space.

'You almost lost the king's taxes to a GIRL!' Sparrow scoffed, roaring back, before becoming more dubious. 'Are you sure you didn't imagine it?'

'I most certainly did not!'

'You're telling me you and your men were almost beaten by a female cutthroat?'

'Listen!' Not caring for Sparrow's pitying expression, Elin picked up the jug from the desk and poured them both a drink. 'Tell me, would you still say that Scathlock serves the best ale in Lichfield?'

All the uncertainty caused by the latest delivery of bad news was temporarily suspended, as Sparrow took a long draught from his tankard. 'I would!'

'And would you still think that if I told you that it was Scathlock's *daughter* who just tried to rob me using a longbow?'

'Is it agreed?'

'Aye, Robin,' Little John was the first to nod, the other outlaws following in turn.

Taking his dagger from his belt and holding the blade up so it shone in the firelight, Will Scarlet growled, 'Can't stand taxmen.'

An almost imperceptible grunt of approval from Nasir sealed the plan.

'Very well then.' Robin looked towards Tuck, who was warming his toes on the opposite side of the camp fire. 'He travelled south from the Newark Road last time, didn't he?'

'He did. Via Lichfield,' Tuck chuckled, 'We stopped him at the crossroads from Newark that leads towards Nottingham, and the occasion before that we greeted him on Aldbury bridge.'

'We can't wait for him at either of those places this time.' Marion weighed an apple in her palm, as she thought aloud. 'Rumour has it that the sheriff has positioned lookouts at the Newark crossroads now, and Elin is bound to be wary of the bridge we used first time around.'

'Wherever we do it,' Will stared into the flames, the orange glow they gave out a stark contrast against the dark of the cool evening, 'we need to be careful. I can't stand that smarmy Welshman, but he ain't stupid. Marion is right—we need a new place to grab him. We need to assume he's learned.'

'Learned *what?*' Much looked up at his friend.

'Not to come without some sort of guard. He'd be stupid to come alone this time, and like I said, he might be a toad of a man but he ain't stupid.'

'I agree.' Robin brushed a blonde hair behind his ear. 'So, where should we relieve him of his money this time?'

Laughter echoed around the tavern, drowning out the steady crackle of the fire in the grate, the constant glug of ale, and the hum of bickering chatter that flowed through the bar.

Narrowly avoiding having a tray of used vessels knocked out of her hands by two rowdy drunks getting overexcited by the prospect of another drink, Fira wove her way between the tables.

Normally she flitted around her father's domain at speed, exchanging friendly, albeit occasionally begrudging, smiles with his customers—doing her best to get through another day and night of work without betraying the fact that she'd rather be almost anywhere else in the world. That evening, however, Fira was barely managing to raise a grin. Her mind seethed with resentment and anger at having let Elin not just escape with the tax money, but also see her face.

She was also afraid.

'Come on, girl, move a little faster, I need those tankards!'

Hauled out of her introspection by her father's harrying, Fira snatched three more empty mugs from a nearby table and plonked them onto her tray. 'I'm going as fast as I can!'

Scathlock pursed his lips as he regarded his daughter, keeping his gaze fixed on her as he called, 'Lia! Help Fira, will you?'

Dashing out from behind the bar and hastening to her friend's side, Lia whispered, 'You okay?'

'What do *you* think? If that Welshman or either of his scum guards recognised me…'

Lia glimpsed anxiously over her shoulder. 'Surely Sparrow would have been here by now if Elin reported you?'

'Maybe.' Fira picked up one more tankard as they sidled through the drinkers towards the bar. 'I didn't like the taunting look he gave me as he rode off.'

Scooping a handful of empty jugs up from where they'd been discarded, Lia muttered, 'What will we do? Give up?'

'Give up? No way!' Shaking out her long wavy red hair, Fira spoke quietly, even though almost everyone was too full of her father's ale to pay much heed to what the barmaids were saying to each other. 'But it might be a good idea if we lay low for a while.'

Lia flicked her pigtail over her shoulder. 'I hate that we didn't get the tax money back.'

'Me too. If my uncle can do it, then so can—' Fira broke off as a customer jarred her elbow, sending the tankard she had just lifted off her tray crashing to the ground, smashing it to pieces.

Scathlock rounded on his daughter, 'What the hell is the matter with you tonight, girl? That's a perfectly good mug gone!'

Lia immediately knelt to the floor to pick up the pieces, 'I'll sort it.'

Taking Fira by the elbow, Scathlock marched his daughter to the far end of the bar, taking no heed of the jeering from his regulars, who were ever hopeful for a bit of drama to add some excitement to their day.

'You've been distracted all evening! I don't pay you to—'

'You don't pay me at all, Father!'

Not rising to this frequently-made complaint, Scathlock stacked some of the dirty tankards into a large barrel ready for washing while he talked. 'Since you got in from the market you've had a temper on you that would make your uncle proud!'

Fira snorted, 'Oh yeah, good old Uncle Will. *His* temper doesn't get criticised, does it? It's viewed as something to praise!' Taking the drying cloth her father thrust at her, she spoke faster. '*He's* allowed to be moody, just because he's a famous outlaw!'

Scathlock banged a tankard so hard against the bar that it was a miracle it didn't crack. 'Don't you go believing a word of it, child! Yes, he may be famous—infamous, more like—but that hot head of his still gets him into trouble! If you hadn't been in Pipehall helping Adam with the brewing last time the outlaws were here, you'd have seen as much for yourself.' He gave a short bark of laughter as he recalled his brother. 'Uncle Will actually threw Robin Hood through the hen-house roof! They fought right through Lichfield, they did.'

Fira's ire cooled in the face of her curiosity. 'Really? But they're friends!'

'What's *that* got to do with it? I'm his brother and I've still got scars from fights I had with Will when I was a young'un.' Turning to serve a customer, Scathlock chuckled. 'Your uncle could argue himself into fighting an abbot—actually, he has!'

Using her cloth to wipe up a slick of ale from the bar, Fira grumbled, 'Well, I'm fed up with hearing about him and his friends. Robin Hood this, Robin Hood that! We're *miles* from Sherwood, and we still have to put up with the stupid ballads about what they get up to. What about *our* people? We all need help too, but do you see your brother coming to stop us being taxed to death?'

Before her father could reply, Fira threw down the cloth. 'I'm going to get some air!'

'Get back here, girl; there's ale to pour!'

'Pour it yourself.'

As Fira stalked off, slamming the tavern door behind her, Scathlock shook his head. 'You moan about your uncle, Fira, but you two are like peas in a pod!'

CHAPTER TWO

Robert de Rainault, High Sheriff of Nottingham, chewed thoughtfully on a strip of roasted pork as he regarded the Captain of the Guard.

'You sent for me, my lord.'

'I did, Captain.' The sheriff leant forward, waving his pork-skewered knife absentmindedly in front of him. 'While Gisburne is away playing at being a pilgrim in Canterbury, I am depending on you to make sure that the Crown's tax money actually reaches the coffers here in the castle, prior to the king's men coming for it next week.'

'I understand, my lord.'

'*Do* you indeed?' The sheriff flicked the remaining slither of meat off his knife and into the fire with a grimace. 'That pork is foul!'

'You wish me to remonstrate with the cook, my lord?'

'I wish to eat anything but pork! It's been non-stop pork for weeks, and do you know what that dolt of a cook said when I complained?'

'No, my lord.'

'He said I wasn't to worry, because that night we were having boar!'

Only just managing not to smile, the captain said nothing, experience telling him that it was best to say nothing unless forced otherwise.

'Last month it was non-stop rabbit! What's wrong with a bit of variety, man?'

'Nothing at all, my lord.'

'Try telling that to the cook! He thinks a change every four weeks or so *is* variety!'

Taking refuge in his goblet of claret, De Rainault got back to the point. 'That Welsh tax collector is due soon. I believe he is an acquaintance of yours, Captain.'

'I've known Elin for many years, my lord.'

'Good. Then you can be the one to look out for him and escort him through the castle gates—with all the tax money in the cart, where it ought to be!'

'Yes, my lord.'

'Send a messenger to Lichfield; that's his resting

place before he comes here, I believe. Find out when he is due, and which way he's coming.'

With a bow of the head, the captain smiled. 'I can already tell you that, my lord.'

'You can?'

'As you say, Elin is a friend of mine. I know when we can expect him, and which direction he'll be coming to avoid those outlaw scum.'

'Do you, Captain?' The sheriff gave a slow smile as he stabbed up another piece of pork. 'Well, you can tell this Elin from me that if he fails this time, friend of yours or not, he'll be dangling on a rope by the end of the week.'

'I've already made him aware of the precarious nature of life, my lord.'

'Have you indeed. How forward thinking of you.' The sheriff indicated to the chair to his left. 'Perhaps you would like to take Gisburne's seat and tell me our Welsh taxman's plans.'

Sparrow's belch made the desk candle gutter.

Elin screwed up his face in distaste as the sheriff's agent took another swig of ale.

18

'It's getting late, Sparrow. I don't intend to travel on with the tax money tonight. Sherwood in the daylight is bad enough, but at night…'

Taking no notice of Elin, Sparrow grumbled disconcertingly into his ale. 'You know, you could be right… if we could catch this chit in the act, the sheriff might let me replace Ambrose. He was…' A hiccup exploded from his lips, making Sparrow belch again before carrying on as if nothing had happened '…a good man. Wrote good, Ambrose did… Clerk, he was… My cousin too…'

Used to Sparrow's drink-lubricated diction, a comparatively sober Elin gave up any chance of being offered a bed for the night any time soon and poured himself some more ale.

'I almost left after Ambrose went—almost went after my cousin—but there was no one suitable to take over…' Sparrow hiccupped again, '…I need to prove to the sheriff that I'm good at my job, and—'

This time Elin interrupted, an idea forming in his mind. 'If you could use Fira's capture to lure her uncle out of Sherwood… and maybe… his friends as well, can you imagine how pleased De Rainault would be?'

Sparrow sat up so quickly that he sloshed some liquid over the side of his cup. 'Yes! That's it—

Ohhh… if I could capture Robin Hood… think of that! Sir Guy of Gisbog would be so cross we did what he keeps failing to do, his neck would go all red! That'd be worth it on its own!'

'You mean Sir Guy of *Gisburne?*'

'That's him—no sense of… *hic*… humour.'

'You're the sheriff's representative, for Heaven's sake!' Sipping his ale, Elin went to lean in closer to Sparrow before, fearing another belch, he thought better of it and sat back again. 'You can't let an innkeeper's daughter get the better of you!'

'Ummm…' A shadow crossed Sparrow's face. 'Maybe I should just arrest her. At least I'd have *one* arrest to please the sheriff.'

The humiliation of his last two rides through Sherwood, when Hood's followers had relieved him of the tax money, rang in Elin's ears as he expounded his plan for revenge. 'But if you were to use the girl, you might be able to capture all of Robin Hood's gang… or maybe just *one* of them…. Will Scarlet is the most feared of Hood's men… at least, he frightens me.'

Sparrow pulled a face. 'You should have seen him when he was a child!'

Not wasting time asking Sparrow to elaborate on his childhood memories, Elin said, 'Then it's agreed. You should use the ill-thought-out actions of Scathlock's daughter to imprison her uncle.'

'Yeah… we'll need one of them things—umm… what d'ya call 'em?'

Elin looked a bit confused. 'What things?'

'I knows!' said Sparrow, triumphantly, his brain kicking in, 'A plan!'

Elin resisted the urge to applaud, now Sparrow had managed to grasp what he'd been saying. 'Yes. A plan for a trap—a trap to catch them *all.*'

Clumsily placing the tankard he'd had halfway to his lips back down, Sparrow leapt off his stool, his eyes narrowing in suspicion as he tottered around his desk, peering at his guest.

''Ere, you ain't that Gisbinge in disguise, are you?'

'Don't be ridiculous, man!'

Sparrow folded his arms. 'You don't half sound like him. Obsessed with plans and traps, he is.'

Elin's sarcasm oozed out, 'Oh yes, I'm *just* like him; Welsh accent and all!' He slapped his palm on the desk, 'Concentrate, man! Don't you want to win back the sheriff's favour?'

Deflated, the sergeant sank back on his stool. 'Yeah—and catch Robin Hood. De Rainault'd like that… *hic* … But how..?'

'We'll need all the men-at-arms at your disposal. I will lend you my guards as well. They've already fought the girl and her helper once… and survived.' Elin paused, not sure how much of what he was about to say would linger in Sparrow's ale-addled mind. 'Now listen. You are going to imprison the innkeeper.'

A look of pure horror crossed Sparrow's face. 'Imprison Scathlock! We can't!' He broke off and waggled a finger towards Elin, as if he realised he'd just been tricked, and started to laugh instead. 'Oh yeah, good one, Elin… I almost believed you for a minute there.'

'I wasn't joking.'

'But… but… Scathlock serves the finest—'

'—ale in Lichfield! Yes, you've said. *So* many times.' Elin rose from his chair and paced the room. 'But not only is Scathlock also brother to one of the most notorious outlaws in England, his daughter held up a tax collector. *This* tax collector! Time you had a chat with him, don't you think?'

Sparrow could feel himself sobering up fast—too fast—and he didn't like it. 'Well, I—'

'And the second you take him into custody, a messenger will be sent into Sherwood…'

'Sherwood?'

'I'm sure Will Scarlet would appreciate knowing how his family are, don't you? In fact, I think we should send someone now—straight away—to set rumour alight.'

'Now? But we ain't arrested Scathlock yet?'

'True, but if we want Scarlet to come and try and save him, then the sooner he gets 'ere, the sooner this will all be over. Yes?'

'Suppose that makes sense.'

'Good.' Elin got to his feet. 'I suggest you speak to your men. One of them needs to get into Sherwood tonight!'

Sparrow grabbed the jug off his desk, and gulped down the remaining ale, without bothering to pour it into his tankard first.

Waking with the light of dawn, Will Scarlet wasn't surprised to see that Little John was no longer lying under the tree where he normally slept.

He'll have gone to Meg. Biting back the bitter tang of jealousy, Will sighed. He would never begrudge his friend some happiness, but so often he wished that Elana had…

Jumping to his feet, not allowing his mind to dwell on what ifs, Scarlet joined Tuck by the fire.

'Ready for a day helping out in Wickham, Scarlet?'

'Handing out money so they can pay their taxes, before we steal it back again? Yeah, why not.'

'No need to be so cynical.' Tuck passed his friend a bowl. 'Here, eat something. You're always less grumpy once you've eaten.'

Will grinned. 'No, I ain't.'

As everyone gathered around the fire, Robin asked, 'Is the money ready to take to the villagers, Tuck?'

'It is. I've counted it into separate purses—but there's only just enough. We'll need to make sure we get more soon.'

'Thank you, Tuck.' Robin took a bowl of pottage, left over from their supper the night before. 'If we split up, then we can cover a few villages between us.'

Marion nodded, 'If we head to Wickham last, we can help Edward with the cabbages.'

'Oh great,' Will tutted, 'If I'd wanted to grow vegetables then…'

'Then *you* can go to Papplewick first.' Tuck threw a purse of coins at Will. 'It's the furthest away.

By the time you get back to Wickham, most of the hard work will be done.'

'Hang on, I didn't say I was afraid of hard work. I just said... what I meant was... it's a hell of a walk and I ain't woken up yet.'

Jumping up, Much said, 'I'll come with you, Will.'

Smiling, Robin inclined his head. 'Right then, Marion and I will go to Calverton. Nasir, I'd like you to go to Waterford. John is already at Wickham, so he can make a start on helping with the planting. We have a day or so before the tax collector reaches Sherwood, so we can visit the other villages tomorrow.'

'That's good.' Much beamed as he turned to Will. 'Shall we go, then?'

'I suppose so. But after I've eaten me breakfast.'

CHAPTER THREE

Fira sat on the floor of the tavern's storeroom, her knees tucked beneath her chin, her arms wrapped around her bent legs. Next to her was Lia, resting against the uneven wooden wall; her face was pale, her body shaking slightly from the cold draught that shot through the gap beneath the door.

After a long silence, Fira glanced at her friend. 'This is all my fault.'

'*Our* fault.'

Tearing a chunk of bread from the loaf she'd taken from the kitchen for her breakfast, Fira passed it to her friend.

'Thanks, Lia, but it was my idea. I'm just glad *you* weren't recognised. I need to find a tunic with a more reliable hood.'

They chewed their food in silence for a while before Fira threw down the loaf in frustration. 'If I hadn't convinced myself that we could help the people... Oh, what's the point!'

Lia rescued the bread from the dirty floor, brushed off any dirt it might have acquired, and gave it back to Fira. 'You need to eat.'

'Not hungry.'

'Don't go all self-pitying on me, it doesn't suit you.' Lia nibbled some of her food. 'Anyway, we *have* helped! We got the money off those two men who'd robbed that old lady last week, *and* we helped that little boy when he got lost up by the crossroads in the winter, and—'

'It's not the same as being able to give people their tax money back though, is it?' Fira ate quietly, before the fear that had been gnawing at her since their return from Pipehall Wood escaped from her lips in a frightened whisper, 'What if they hang my father because of what we did?'

'They wouldn't—they can't,' Lia spoke mid-chew. '*He* didn't do anything. They can't hang him for what *we* did!'

Not for the first time, Fira was amazed by her friend's naivety. She was as brave as anything, but the realities of life often seemed to pass Lia by.

'That horrible Welsh tax collector *must* be behind this. He must have told Sparrow he saw me. I bet they think I'll try to save my father. Then they'll capture me too—and probably hang us *both*.'

Lia gulped, the action making her swallow her mouthful prematurely. 'Like he's bait in a trap!' She took a drink, trying to shift the lump of bread that had wedged in her throat. 'If that's true, then what do we do?'

A sharp breeze blew under the door, making Fira stand up. 'Rescue him, of course—but… carefully.' She exhaled. 'I need time to think—there must be some way we can save my father without getting caught too.'

Fira began to tidy up the storeroom from where, the previous evening, she and Lia had run in and out fetching supplies for their customers before her father had been dragged away in a riotous cloud of confusion.

'Lia, I want you to run the tavern. I'm going back to Pipehall Wood while I work out what to do.'

'But…'

Fear made Fira snap at her friend. 'I can't stay, it's not safe. If I hadn't hidden when Sparrow's men took my father, I'd probably have been arrested too.

I don't want to go, but I *must*. Can you think of a better idea?'

'Yes! Sticking together! I'll come too.'

Fira ran a hand through her tangle of red hair, freeing the pigtail that had started to become loose. 'There's nothing I'd like more, but we must keep the tavern going. There's got to be something for my father to come back to. Who knows how long it'll be until we get him home.'

If he comes home.

All the way to Papplewick, Much had been talkative; however, now their task was complete—and the money the village needed to pay the king's taxes had been delivered—he had lapsed into silence.

Will glanced at his friend as they wove their way back through the trees towards Wickham. His face was drawn, and Will suspected he was battling the need to cry. 'You alright, Much?'

'Yeah.'

'Uh-huh.' Striding forwards, Will said no more. He knew what ailed Much. It hadn't been that many months since he'd lost his friend Kate, a resident of

Papplewick, and—since then—Much had changed; the last vestiges of the boy had turned, more markedly than ever, into a man.

He always said she was just a friend… maybe that's his way of coping. If he says she was more than that, then…

Will stopped his thoughts before they could develop further. There was no point in trying to find the right thing to say, or offering to help his friend. There were no right words, and nothing helped. He knew that better than anyone.

It wasn't until they reached the narrow pathway that led them into the clearing which denoted the village of Wickham that Much spoke. 'I hopes they've made a start on the planting. I'm not that keen on cabbages.'

Will chuckled. 'Don't let Tuck 'ear you say that.'

'Suppose Meg'll have had John up before dawn. They'll have been hard at work hours ago.'

'Serves him right for sloping off to see her in the night,' Will snorted.

'Yeah,' Much chuckled, his usual good humour restored now they were getting nearer to their friends.

Edward of Wickham wiped the sweat from his brow as he rested against the table, gratefully taking the pitcher of ale that his wife, Alison, passed to him.

'Are you sure, Edward?' Robin asked.

'I'm sure.'

John hugged Meg to his side. 'Scarlet isn't going to like it.'

'To be fair, John, Scarlet rarely likes *anything*,' Edward grimaced. 'Although I do have another piece of news that might make him smile.'

'Go on,' Robin leaned his muddy hands on the table.

'The word around Nottingham is…' Edward broke off as the outlaws turned as one, staring towards the forest. 'What is it?' he asked, worriedly.

His question was immediately answered, when he spotted Much and Will emerging from the trees.

'How do you all do that?' Edward marvelled.

'Practice,' Nasir smiled.

'Might as well wait until they are here and then you can tell us your news when we're all together, Edward.' Marion gestured towards their approaching colleagues. 'They made good time from Papplewick.'

Much and Will hadn't quite reached the others, when Will called out, 'What's happened?'

Robin nodded towards Edward. 'Word has reached Nottingham—word from Lichfield.'

'Lichfield?'

Not missing the sharpness to Will's tone, Edward didn't waste time. 'I was in Nottingham early. There was man in the market. He was buying some bread to...'

'I don't care what he was buying. What did he say?'

'Alright, Will,' Marion scolded. 'Go on, Edward.'

Unruffled, Edward continued. 'He was tasked with taking word to the castle. Scathlock has been arrested by the sheriff's sergeant.'

'He's *what?*'

Robin put an arm on Will's shoulder, as he addressed Wickham's headman. 'Did you recognise this messenger, Edward?'

'No. No, I'm afraid not.'

Marion watched Will carefully as she asked, 'Do you think it was true? Or was it just rumour?'

'Rumour or not, it's got the folk of Nottingham gossiping. Although, word is, the messenger had other news for the sheriff, so...'

'So it *might* not be true... but it probably is,' Meg chipped in.

'Thanks. Very helpful,' Will scowled, earning

32

himself a warning stare from Little John. 'Was any of this rumour saying what my brother has done, Edward?'

'The messenger claimed he didn't know why he'd been taken.'

'Taken where?' Much asked.

'To Lichfield gaol, where the hell do you think he'd be taken, Much!' Will snapped.

'Oh, yeah. Of course,' Much muttered.

Closing his eyes, exhaling in a rush of anger, Will turned to his friend and ruffled his hair. 'I didn't mean to snap. Sorry, Much.'

'That's alright.'

Wishing, not for the first time, that he could be as forgiving as Much, Scarlet swivelled round to face Robin. 'I 'ave to go.'

'We have the king's tax man passing through Sherwood any day now. Could be tomorrow, even.' Robin shook his head. 'We need you here, Scarlet.'

'And my brother needs me there!' Will scowled, 'What would *you* do?'

'I'd do what was best for everyone.'

'Yeah, you would, wouldn't you. And it'd work out alright—always does for you.' Will scrubbed a hand through his hair in frustration, 'But I ain't *you!*'

Little John looked to Edward. 'Before Will and Much arrived, you were about to tell us something else you overheard.'

'Elin, the Welshman.'

'The tax collector,' Robin asked, 'you know when we can expect him?'

'You were right, it's soon. Tomorrow. The day after, at the latest.'

'Do you know which way he'll be coming, Edward?' John asked.

'I don't, but I *did* learn something else of interest.' Edward took another sip of ale. 'Turns out, Elin's only managed to keep his job—despite you relieving him of the money twice before—because he has friends in high places.'

Scarlet's disbelief was clear. 'That man has *friends?*'

Nasir looked directly at Edward. 'The sheriff?'

'Not *that* high. Not Gisburne either.'

'Who then?' Will snapped.

'The Captain of the Guard, no less,' Edward smiled at Robin. 'I thought that might be helpful.'

Herne's son nodded slowly. 'You thought right. Thank you, Edward.'

34

While stretching his arms up over his head, Elin threw his legs over the side of the rickety cot upon which he'd slept—or tried to sleep. Thinking longingly of his bed back in London, a place that had been home for more years than he'd ever spent in his native Monmouth, he glared at the slumbering figure on the other side of the room.

Sparrow was sound asleep, snoring like a boar, his belly rising and falling like a pair of inflated bellows. Whatever misgivings he'd had about sending a messenger to Nottingham to proclaim that Scathlock had been taken prisoner—three hours prior to the arrest having actually taken place—had all been easily been wiped away by the steady application of the felon's ale.

Splashing his face with cold water from a barrel in the corner of the room, Elin wondered if Sparrow slept in his office because he had nowhere else to go, or if it was because he was usually so drunk by bedtime that he found it easier—and safer—to simply fall onto one of the two cots on the far side of the room.

Perhaps this one belonged to the much-missed Ambrose, Elin mused as he retrieved his cloak from the cot. *He liked a drop or two of Scathlock's finest as well.*

Not bothering to wake Sparrow, Elin headed to the door. It was time to set the second half of his plan into motion.

CHAPTER FOUR

Wrapping his cloak tighter around his broad shoulders, Will Scarlet marched into Sherwood. He was deep beneath the cover of the trees before he heard a sound behind him that could only have been Much.

'What do you want?'

'It's only a rumour, Will.'

'I don't like rumours.'

'Well, no—nor do I—but that must be all this is. Can't be true, can it?'

Will's angry expression focussed on Much as he came to an abrupt stop. 'Why would a messenger have been sent to tell the sheriff if it wasn't true?'

'Yeah, alright, um…'

As Will stomped off again, Much called after him. 'Where you going?'

'Where do you *think* I'm going? To Lichfield, of course! I don't care what Robin says, my brother needs me, so I'm going.' Ducking under a low-hanging branch, Will increased his speed. 'S'pose I'll be able to if I can get me old boots back.'

Jogging to keep up, Much asked, 'Boots?'

A slow smile crossed Will's face, temporarily wiping away his concern. 'Yeah, the boot seller in Lichfield—she took me boots the last time I visited. Gave me new ones... Rosanna... she was quite a lass, she...' The moment of recollection dissolved as Scarlet remembered the reason why he was heading towards Lichfield this time. 'Never mind that! If that rat of a sheriff's man has taken my brother prisoner, then I've got to make sure he's freed again.'

Glancing anxiously over his shoulder towards Wickham, Much ventured, 'Shouldn't we tell Robin?'

'No.'

'But you left while we was doing the cabbages—he won't have seen you go.'

Rounding on Much, his temper ready to break, Will grasped hold of the younger man's tunic, but quickly let go when he saw his worried expression. 'Look Much, if I tell Robin, he'll want to come. I'm not leaving Sherwood unprotected because my family needs me. Anyway, Robin can't spare both of us, not with that lowlife tax gatherer due to ride through Sherwood any day now.'

Scuffing a boot against the forest floor, Much mumbled, 'I suppose so. You'll take care of yourself, won't you, Will?'

With a wink, Will grinned, 'When don't I?'

Despite the cloak she wore, Fira still shivered as she travelled the pathways of Pipehall Woods, her chill only partly from the early morning temperatures. Fear for her father, and—if she was honest—for herself and Lia, sent repeated quivers of unease through her slight frame.

Wishing her friend was with her, but knowing it would have been too dangerous to have Lia come along as well, Fira was already tiring. Sleep had evaded her the night before, and her muddled mind couldn't concentrate.

I need to stop, rest and think. That's what Robin Hood would do—he'd make sure he had a plan.

Thus resolved, Fira changed direction, taking a barely visible track to her right, which she knew led to an old tree with a partly hollow trunk. The perfect place to sit out of sight, close her eyes, and decide what to do next.

Rescue my father, clear his name, and somehow convince Sparrow that it wasn't me that Elin saw.

Fira groaned.

Not even Robin Hood could do all that—and he has people to help him.

Much hadn't been able to settle.

Robin had been furious when Much had told him that Will had gone to Lichfield. It had taken some firm but wise words from Marion to get Robin to calm down, and—even after that—there was an atmosphere that hung around the village.

Much had been glad to return to his row of cabbage sets, but as he'd worked, all he'd been able to think about was Will, and how he had no one to help him if things went wrong. And—instinct told Much—that's exactly what would happen.

Especially if his temper gets the better of 'im. Then he's a danger to himself as well as everyone else...

Glancing apprehensively towards where Robin

and John were hard at work, Much sidled towards Edward.

'You're going to go after Will, aren't you.'

Much's mouth fell open. 'How did you know that?'

'Because I've known you a long time,' Edward smiled, before waving a hand towards a bag at the end of the row of vegetables. 'There's some bread and a full pouch of water in there. Take it. Help Will and then get back to Sherwood as fast as you can.'

'Robin's going to be angry with me, isn't he?'

'Probably, but he'll be more cross with the fact that he wants to help everyone, and can't.'

'How do you mean?'

'He wanted to go after Will, he'll want to follow you too. But if he does that, then there'll be no one to stop Elin and to get the villagers' money back.'

'So he has to choose.'

Edward was solemn as he stared across the furrows to where the other outlaws toiled. 'He always has to choose, and the choices are never easy.'

'I'm glad I ain't Robin.' Picking up Edward's bag, Much thanked his friend. 'Can you tell Robin I'm sorry, and I'll bring Will back with me soon.'

Edward smiled. 'Of course I will. Herne protect you, Much the Miller's Son.'

'Oh, ah—thanks. And I 'ope he protects you too.'

Taking the same route he and his friends had travelled when they'd tried to persuade Will Scarlet to rejoin them, after Robert of Huntingdon had taken on the mantle of Herne's Son, Much hurried through Sherwood. With each mile, he hoped that Will would have stopped for a rest, so he had a chance of catching him up before he reached Lichfield's boundary...

But if he hasn't stopped, at least I know where he'll go—the inn. He's bound to go there first to...

Much's thoughts stopped in time with his steps. A change in the light between the trees a little way ahead of him told him he wasn't alone. Freeing the bow from his shoulder, he fixed an arrow to the string, but kept the weapon lowered as he edged forwards—before unnotching the arrow again and running forwards, a smile on his face.

'Can't believe you didn't hear me coming.'

Hiding the split second of fear he experienced, followed by annoyance at himself for not paying attention to his surroundings, Will mumbled, 'Course I heard you! Like a frightened pheasant you were.'

'Oh.'

Feeling guilty at the disappointment in Much's voice, Will slowed down so his friend could fall into step with him 'Why are you 'ere, anyway? I told you to stay with the others.'

'You might need my help. I left a message in Wickham. Edward will tell Robin after he's finished toiling the soil.'

Feeling bad that he'd already sniped at Much several times that day, and that—because of him—Much had left the others a man down, Will said, 'But Robin's going to need you.'

'He's got John and Nasir and Tuck *and* Marion.'

'But he ain't got us! He ain't got *you*, Much!' Will slowed his pace. 'You're better with a bow than any of us but Robin these days.'

Much's eyebrows shot up in surprise. 'Am I?'

'You are.'

'Oh,' Much faltered, 'Had I better go back then?'

Will walked faster. 'It's up to you.'

'I'll come with you.' Hurrying to keep up, Much couldn't help but glance back the way he'd come, an image of the other outlaws (getting cross with him for leaving without telling them) growing more vivid in his mind. 'We won't be long anyway—will we?'

'Hope not.' Accepting that he now had a companion, Scarlet gestured to the bag Much carried. 'What's in there?'

'Edward gave me some bread and water for the journey.'

'Good man, that Edward.' Will gave his friend a sideways look as they strode along. 'Much…'

'Yeah?'

'I'm glad you're coming.'

'Just because I got food?'

'Why else?' Scarlet grinned, teasingly.

CHAPTER FIVE

Elin's expression could only be described as devious, as he was joined by his same two guards that Fira and her companion had fought the previous day.

'You two have some work ahead of you to save your reputations.' Elin looked sternly from one guard to the other. 'I don't intend to tell the Sheriff of Nottingham exactly how we were attacked, but I am sure you can imagine his reaction if I did.'

A mumbling 'Yes, sir' came from the guards, in turn, as they stood under the cover of the trees, on the edge of Pipehall Village.

'The last thing I need, especially after Hood's men took the taxes twice before, is another blow to my reputation.' Elin glared at each guard in turn. 'What are your names?'

Surprised that the tax man had bothered asking, the taller of the two men, replied first. 'James.'

'Simon.'

'Well then, James and Simon,' Elin gestured towards the wood behind them, 'I arrived here not long after first light. Fira Scathlock has been moving through the trees, from thicket to coppice, all morning.'

'You've actually seen her?' James had imagined Will Scarlet's niece to be as cunning as her uncle. 'And she hasn't seen you?'

'You don't get to survive as one of King John's tax collectors if you can't blend into the undergrowth without being seen.'

'Like an outlaw,' James grimaced.

'Exactly—know your enemy and work out how to think like them.' Elin's expression was grim. 'I'd guess that she's been hiding in the woods all night.'

James rested a hand on the handle of the sword at his belt. 'You think she'll sneak into the village to find food?'

'I would, if I were her,' The tax gatherer agreed. 'She's keeping her hood up, even though she believes herself unobserved. The girl is learning.'

The men remained silent as they continued to watch for any movement between the trees. After a while, Elin grunted at Simon. 'Will you be able to fight with that wounded leg?'

Flushing crimson, still embarrassed at being injured, Simon stood to attention, biting back the wince of pain he felt in his leg as he did so. 'It's only a flesh wound. Well-bound. I can fight.'

'So I should think. I can just imagine the sheriff's face if I end up having to tell him that the guards he gave me to protect the king's money were beaten by two women!'

'We don't know the other one was a woman,' Simon protested.

'Fira has a friend with whom she works in the tavern. I'd put a king's ransom on it being her.'

'Oh.' Simon's cheeks coloured darker. 'You said you wouldn't tell the sheriff.'

'I said I don't *intend* to—sometimes he leaves a man with no choices.'

Simon was about to speak again when Elin had put a finger to his own lips and pointed into the wood. They only had to wait a minute until they all saw Fira flit between two clumps of trees, before lowering herself to the ground.

After a while, Simon muttered, 'She's just sat there. We could take her now rather than risking another fight.'

'Risking?' Elin shook his head and hissed, 'You talk like a coward. She's just a woman!'

'With respect, sir,' James said, 'she is not. She is a Scathlock, and both she and her friend—whoever they were—fight well. Very well.'

Acknowledging the fact with a curt dip of his head, Elin kept his eyes on their quarry. 'Fira's not the prize. She's the bait.'

Simon frowned. 'I thought Scathlock was the bait?'

The Welshman crossed his arms over his ample belly. 'Who said there was only one trap?'

Backing into the shadows to make sure they were not seen; Elin threw a sack at the guards. 'There are clothes inside. Put them on. That girl tried to disgrace me. She needs to be taught a lesson, but the sheriff's expecting me in Nottingham, and only a very stupid man would delay with the Crown's taxes. You two will have to do the teaching without me.' Grateful that the guards appeared to have rather more intelligence than he'd first credited them with, Elin was pleased to see both men comply without question. 'If that girl wants to be Robin Hood, she'll need outlaws to lead, won't she.'

'You have a plan for us to carry out, sir?' James yanked a dirty brown tunic over his head.

'I do,' Elin grinned. 'Let me explain...'

Jumping off the horses they'd stolen from two unwitting members of the sheriff's garrison who had, unwisely, been patrolling the outer edge of the forest on their own, neither outlaw wanted to admit that they were relieved to have reached the road into Lichfield without encountering any real trouble— and without having to walk.

Much chuckled as he smoothed his horse's neck, soothingly. 'Bet you's hoping the lady boot seller is home. No wonder you're not complaining about having to walk to Lichfield!'

Unable to prevent the beam that crossed his face whenever he remembered Rosanna, Will put out a hand for the pouch that now hung at Much's belt. 'Well, these new boots still ain't broken in. I want me old one's back.' He paused, and then added, 'Got any water left?'

'Here.'

Will took a glug of liquid. 'Much, I ain't sure what we're going to find when we get to Lichfield, and... if that idiot of a sheriff's man is still there...'

'Sparrow.'

'That's him… well, just be careful, alright. If my brother really *has* got himself arrested, I've no idea yet how we'll free him.'

Unable to resist the chance to tease his friend, Much suggested, 'You could always ask the lady boot seller—*she* might have an idea.'

'I should never have told you about her.' Will nudged Much in the ribs. ''Ere, Rosanna might have a sister for you!'

'Will!' Much blushed bright red.

Even if the position of the sun in the sky hadn't told her it was almost noon, Fira's stomach was making the point for her. She'd left the tavern in such a hurry that she'd not taken any food with her, and although relieved to still be at liberty, Fira knew she'd have to decide what to do next soon—and whatever that was, it needed to involve the acquiring of food and drink.

Uncle Will would never have gone out without supplies.

Checking all was quiet around her, she cursed

her foolishness as she massaged some feeling back into her cold cramped limbs.

Adam will give me some food. He's a friend; been providing ale for us for years.

Fira took a few hesitant steps before pausing again, wondering what she'd say about her unexpected appearance in the village at a time when everyone would be expecting her to be keeping the tavern going for her father. She knew there was no hope whatsoever of word of her father's arrest not having reached Pipehall.

No one knows what I've been doing... I'll say I've been for walk and lost track of time while worrying about my father.

Once she reached the very edge of Pipehall Wood, where it backed onto the village, Fira waited under the cover of the trees, observing the residents moving around. After a while she spotted her quarry.

Adam.

Taking a deep breath, hoping she looked as if she'd just come from the tavern and hadn't been wandering the woods for hours, she raised a hand as she hailed him. 'Good day, Adam.'

Spinning round, Adam took a moment to work out who was addressing him. 'Fira? Is that you under that cloak?'

'Yes, I...' Cursing her foolishness at forgetting she was in a cloak she'd taken from her father's chest, Fira got no further. A flurry of movement behind her made her spin round. 'What the...?'

James spoke without a flicker of unease as he patted Fira on the back as if they were old friends. 'Sorry Fira, we took a wrong turn. I bet you thought you'd lost us!'

While Fira stared at James in bewilderment, Simon stood directly behind her, a blade in the small of her back as he whispered into her ear. 'I'm sure you can feel my knife at your back. Pretend to know us, or you'll never see your father again.'

'Fira, are you alright?' Adam hurried forward. 'Do you know these men?'

The prick of the sharp blade against her back reinforced her unexpected associates intentions clear, as Simon smiled at Adam. 'Course she does, friends of your uncle's aren't we, Fira.'

'Umm... yeah, they're friends of Uncle Will.'

Running over to the village barn, James opened the door. 'Yeah, and ole Scarlet don't like what the sheriff's man has done to 'er father. He's asked us to look after his niece until Scathlock's released. Told us to find a safe place to let her lie low. This barn looks perfect.'

'Hang on a minute.' Adam followed the two newcomers as they towed Fira along in their wake. 'We need that barn for…'

Before Adam could finish speaking, a confused Fira found herself thrust inside the barn, with Adam at her side, and Simon and James on their heels.

'What's going on…?' Fira's words died on her lips as the barn door was bolted shut behind them.

Adam tried to reach past James to get to the door, but the knives both men held in their hands halted his efforts.

'What are you doing?' Fira snarled. 'How do you know my uncle? You aren't Robin Hood's men.'

'We are.' The dull throb in his leg was making Simon irritable. 'Robin lets anyone good at fighting join him… if they hate the sheriff enough.'

'No he doesn't.' The hairs on the back of Fira's neck stood up, every instinct in her screaming that something was very wrong. However, there was no time for her to yell for help. At the top of his voice, so that the villagers they could hear assembling outside the barn heard him, Simon bellowed towards the wooden-slatted door.

'People of Pipehall! On the advice of Will Scarlet, Fira Scathlock has taken Adam the brewer hostage! She has a knife to his throat.'

Hammering on the inside of the barn door, Adam cried to his captors, 'Let me out! Don't you know that without me, there's no ale!'

James put a hand over Adam's mouth, before shouting, 'Take heed, peasants! Think before you act! The sheriff's man, Sparrow, has Scathlock—and Scathlock's daughter here has the brewer. Until her father is freed, she will keep Adam under the blade of her knife. And *we* are going to make sure not one of you tries to stop her!'

As a horrified Fira listened to what was being done in her uncle's name, Simon added, 'Which of you is brave enough to tell that idiot Sparrow he must free the innkeeper before Lichfield's ale supply runs dry!'

CHAPTER SIX

The sheriff tucked into the plate of roast pheasant with an enthusiasm that carried the danger of violent indigestion.

'Captain!' He called across the great hall as he saw his head guard making for the main door.

'My lord?' The soldier immediately changed direction and attended on the sheriff.

'I have pheasant.'

A smile curled at the corner of the captain's lips. 'Yes, my lord.'

'The servant who brought my food told me you had a word with the cook.'

'Yes, my lord.' The captain squared his soldiers, 'You mentioned that a change to a pork diet would be welcome.'

The twin effects of a non-swine related meal and strong claret improving his mood further, the sheriff grinned. 'Extremely welcome.'

'I think I have managed to persuade the cook to make sure you have more variety at meal times. I cannot promise there won't be pork for dinner again soon, though.'

With a dip of his head, the sheriff picked up a roasted pheasant wing. 'It occurs to me that you have been overlooked for far too long, Captain. Once the delivery of the taxes has been successfully dealt with, we should talk about promoting you further.'

As Much and Will walked into the heart of Lichfield, they kept their eyes open, on the constant lookout for trouble.

'We'll go straight to the inn.'

'Not to the boot seller?'

'Family first, Much.'

Much's smile dropped. 'Yeah, sorry. I was only joking.'

Will gave him a pat on the shoulder. 'It's alright Much, I know you were.'

As the two men progressed through Lichfield, passing many of the market stalls and workshops they'd seen on their last visit, they became aware of various groups of townsfolk gossiping along the side of the road.

Suddenly, Much stopped moving. 'Do you hear what they're whispering, Will?'

'It'll just be old women's tattle.' Will didn't pause his stride. 'I'm dying for a drink. Fira'll get some ale for us.'

'Fira?' Much repeated the girl's name as he hurried to Will's side. 'Who's Fira?'

'My niece! Come on…'

Tugging at Will's arm, Much finally got him to stop moving. Looking his friend straight in the eye, he spoke urgently. 'Fira is *your* niece? You never said you had a niece.'

'We don't all flaunt our families, Much!'

'But, Will, you don't understand! Them women back there said…'

'No, Much, you are the one who's not understanding. I ain't interested in a load of old gossips.'

Much tried again, 'Listen…'

'I told you! I'm doing *nothing* until I've had at least one jug of ale!'

Will Scarlet threw back the door to his brother's inn so hard that it slammed against the wall, before swinging shut again. 'Fira! Where are you, girl?'

Already jumpy, Lia flinched, as she spun around. 'Who's asking?'

'Fira's uncle. Who are you?'

Lia put down the pot she'd been wiping, and—with a mix of relief and awe—she asked. 'You're Will Scarlet?'

'Yeah.'

'And I'm Much.'

Will surveyed the suspiciously empty bar. 'And we *still* don't know who you are.'

'Lia.'

'Well, Lia, we've walked a long way and we're dying for a drink.'

Taking comfort in the familiar task of pouring ale, Lia carried two full tankards over to where Fira's uncle and Much had sat down.

'I'm so glad you're here. Fira will be too.'

Will's eyes narrowed. 'Why's the inn empty? I thought Fira would be keeping things going until that idiot Sparrow comes to his senses and frees my brother.'

'You've heard, then?'

'Yeah, we've heard.' Will downed his tankard of ale in one, before wiping his hand across his mouth with an accompanying burp of satisfaction.

'I haven't opened the inn—I'd never cope on my own. Thought I'd get the place clean and ready for when Scathlock returns.' The worry Lia had been trying to hide since her employer had been marched away by four of Sparrow's man—one holding each limb as the innkeeper violently protested in true Scathlock style—was suddenly visible on her face, as she sat with the outlaws. 'But that means they must have made sure you heard—how *did* you hear?'

'Gossip from Nottingham reached Wickham. They're always talking about...'

Will swapped a surprised glance with Much when the young woman interrupted him and began to talk hurriedly to herself. 'Yes... *Wickham*—that's the village most associated with you all...' Lia looked up; her wide hazel eyes fixed on Scarlet. 'Even Nottingham is quite a way from Lichfield for a messenger to have spread word that would reach the villages you and your friends care for already.

Unusual for even rumour to have travelled so fast, don't you think?'

'Now you come to mention it…' Will refilled his mug from the jug Lia had placed on the table. '…that *was* quite fast. Even if they'd had a horse, the chances of…'

'Umm… pardon my interruption, but it all makes sense now…' Lia played her pigtail between her fingers as she thought aloud. 'This must be the tax collector's work. Sparrow is too much of a fool to have come up with anything this sneaky. Oh clever…very clever. He's…'

Will slapped a palm onto the table to break her flow. 'For heaven's sake, girl! You're worse than Herne, talking nonsense! Tell me what's been going on. Now!'

'It was Elin, the Welshman. We tried to stop him. Fira and me—we wanted to take the tax money back.'

Will was incredulous. 'You did *what?*'

Lia lowered her gaze to the floor as she muttered, 'We wanted to help people, like you do. We *have* been helping, but this time…it went wrong.'

Much risked a glance at Will's furrowed expression. 'Elin—is that the taxman Robin and the others are waiting for.'

'He always was a sneaky piece of...' Thinking better of finishing his sentence, Scarlet took another glug of ale instead.

Giving Lia, what he hoped was a comforting smile, Much asked, 'How did it go wrong?'

'Fira's hood fell down. Elin saw her face,' Lia sighed. 'If he hadn't, we'd have been okay—although he'd still have got away. I beat one of the guards, though—Elin had two men hiding in the cart with the money,' She sighed again, 'but Fira's hair is so distinctive—everyone knows her fiery red hair. Soon as she realised her hood was down, she felt vulnerable, I suppose. Lost concentration.'

Will sat up straight. 'Is she hurt?'

'No, but the guards got off with little more than a scratch and Elin rode off with the taxes.'

'You were both lucky,' Much said.

'No.' Lia tilted her chin up proudly. 'We were *unlucky*—the guards were the lucky ones. Normally we'd have knocked them both out, no problem.'

'Her mother, may she rest in peace, didn't name her Fira for nothing.' Will was unable to keep a small smile curl the corner of his lips. 'Where is she, Lia?'

The reply came from Much. 'She's holding the brewer hostage in the village of Pipehall.'

There were two thuds of pottery against the table as Lia fumbled a jug, just as Will thumped down his tankard. They spoke in unison: 'She's *what?*'

'That's what I heard as we came through Lichfield. People were talking about a girl called Fira. If you'd told me you had a niece...'

'I didn't know it was gonna be important, did I?' Suddenly angry again, Will snapped, 'I thought we were coming to free my brother, not sort out the whole family!'

Righting the jug she'd been carrying, Lia looked from one outlaw to the other. 'If you two would stop bickering for one minute!'

Contrite, the men gave Lia their full attention as she topped up their tankards.

'Fira would never hurt Adam—never!'

'Who's Adam?' Much asked.

'The brewer. He's a friend.' Lia gaze roamed over the oddly empty tavern. 'This place would be nothing without his ale.'

Will lifted his tankard. 'Why would people be saying she has kidnapped him?'

'Cos Scathlock's been taken...' Much added, 'I heard them women say that Fira and her outlaws will let Adam go once he's free.'

'Much! Why didn't you tell me at once?'

'I did try. You never gave me a chance to finish a sentence!'

Scarlet raised a hand of acknowledgement. 'Yeah, well... Fira always did have a hot temper. No idea where she gets it from.'

Much's eyebrows shot upwards. 'Seriously?'

'Alright! So perhaps I've got a rough idea,' Will snorted as he knocked back the rest of his ale. 'Lia, why has Sparrow taken my brother?'

'To frighten Fira, maybe. I don't really know. But, umm... the thing is... well—what we did, me and Fira, we did on our own. Just the two of us. We don't work with *anyone* else. So, who are these other outlaws that have Adam and Fira?'

CHAPTER SEVEN

Having explained his plan to Sparrow for the third time, an exasperated Elin checked the tax money was still safe in the back of the cart, where two of Lichfield's finest had been guarding it.

'I *think* I get it,' Sparrow said, 'but what I don't get is why you ain't staying to see Scarlet and Fira Scathlock get captured.'

'I wish I could.' Elin checked the cart's fastenings. 'Believe me, nothing would give me more pleasure than seeing them get their comeuppance, but the Sheriff of Nottingham is expecting me today. I've already delayed too long to help you catch that Scathlock woman.'

'By the time you get to the castle, it'll be late—dark. I ain't drunk enough to have forgotten that you said going through Sherwood at night is a bad idea.'

Reluctant to admit that the sheriff's sergeant was right, Elin put on a show of bravado he didn't quite feel. 'Some of us aren't afraid of the dark. Anyway, I don't reckon that Robin Hood will be expecting to me so late.'

'Maybe not.'

'As long as I get to the castle before midnight, then I'll still be arriving today.'

'But you ain't got your men with you, and I… *hic*… can't spare any; not with all this going on.'

Elin hauled himself up onto the wooden seat from where he could drive the cart. 'I won't need any. Like I said, no outlaw will think I'd be brave enough—or stupid enough—to travel into the forest at night.'

'Maybe not.' Sparrow stroked the horse's mane as he looked up at the tax collector. 'But every outlaw I've ever had the misfortune to meet has been perfectly at home in the dark. I'd get going before the last of the daylight goes, if I were you… just in case you encounter a thief or two out for a walk in the moonlight.'

Not appreciating the observation, Elin countered, 'And if you don't want to be fighting

Will Scarlet in the dark, you'd better get going too,' before he shook the reins and drove the cart out of the guardhouse's stables.

After sending Lia outside to see what she could learn from the gossip that was running rife through the townsfolk about the innkeeper and his daughter, Will had prowled the length of the tavern until she'd returned to share her findings.

As soon as Lia had confirmed that what Much had overheard was accurate, Will had grabbed his sword and dashed out of the tavern.

Leaving his barely-touched tankard of ale behind, Much had trailed his friend through the late afternoon chill. He let Scarlet brood in silence until they reached the boundary of Lichfield, before asking, 'Where are we going?'

'Pipehall Woods.'

'Alright then.'

Privately marvelling at Much's ability to trust that he and their fellow outlaws always knew what they were doing, Scarlet remained trapped in his own thoughts until they were safely under the shelter of the trees. 'What the hell were they thinking? Two young women out here with bows, arrows and swords. Anything could've 'appened to them.'

'They wanted to help people like we do.'

Will tutted as they moved deeper into the wood. 'But it's different for us, Much! If one of us...' Will faltered. 'We know the risks. We survive because we've had practice. They're just kids!'

'They're my age!'

'You know what I mean.' He paused. 'Where the hell did they get weapons like that anyway?'

'Probably stole 'em.'

'That's not helpful, Much!' Will stamped through a thicket of silver birch. 'This is all Robin's fault!'

Offended on Robin's behalf, Much protested, 'He don't even know about this!'

Staring between the trees to his left, Will raged quietly to himself. 'He makes it sound noble, Much! When was risking your life every flippin' day noble? Fira and Lia held up a tax man with bows and arrows! Where do you think they got an idea like that from? *Us! We* are responsible!'

'Yeah—I know—I said, they were just trying to help.'

'And look how that turned out, Much! Now we've gotta help Fira *and* my brother, and I...'

Breaking off, Scarlet kicked a twig out of the way. 'I'm sorry, Much—sometimes this life of ours…'

Understanding how hard his friend found it to express his feelings, Much steered the conversation back to the matter in hand. 'Who do you think these other outlaws are?'

'I know exactly who they are, Much. They're trouble.'

Lapsing back into silence, they snuck forwards. Taking more care with each step they took, they finally neared the far side of the wood that led into Pipehall village.

'It's a trap, isn't it.'

'Of course it's a trap, Much! It's always a trap.' Will quickly mastered his fraying temper and added more thoughtfully, 'But is it a trap for Fira, or for us?'

Much clambered over a fallen tree trunk. 'Should we have let Lia come and help us, like she wanted too?'

'We have enough to worry about without protecting 'er as well.'

'She seemed nice.'

Will gave Much a double take. 'Don't you go falling for her! Last thing we need is you going soppy.'

Much's whole face went pink with embarrassment. 'I only said she was nice!'

'I heard ya.'

'Well, I'm not interested—she's just pretty, that's all.'

Will gave his friend a knowing smile. 'Pretty—yeah, Much, she's very pretty.'

'I bet your boot lady's pretty...'

Robin had barely spoken since Edward had informed him that it wasn't just Will Scarlet who'd left Sherwood.

Now, as they returned to the camp, Tuck bustled around his cooking pots, his belief that everyone thought more calmly on a full stomach propelling him into action.

As Nasir kindled the fire, John headed to where Robin was leaning against a tree trunk, clearly brooding. Knowing he was risking provoking their leader's temper, the big man asked the question he knew the others were thinking. 'Should we get ready to go to Lichfield, then?'

'If we go after them, then the taxes will get to the castle, and we'll never get them back.'

'We could attack the wagon when it comes out

of the castle again,' John suggested, 'when it's on its way to London.'

Robin shook his head. 'You know it'll be too well guarded by then.'

'Too dangerous,' Nasir agreed.

'Aye, I suppose so.' John paused, before tentatively adding, 'But, Will's brother is…'

'I know!' Robin closed his eyes, opening them almost straight away, his tone more measured. 'I know, John, but our first duty is to the people of Sherwood.'

Blowing out a sigh of frustration, Robin turned and walked into the trees, his blond hair standing out amongst the greenery. John went to follow, but Marion intercepted him. A brief wave of a finger was enough to tell John to return to the fire and leave the Hooded Man to her.

Holding out her hand as she approached Robin, Marion said nothing while she waited for him to take it. Then, with a gentle tug, she strolled further away from the camp, towing him in her wake.

'I know you're angry with Will, but you know you'd have done the same thing if the roles were reversed.'

'We need him here. We need them both.'

Seeing the obstinate jut of Robin's chin, Marion

didn't argue. 'We do, but right now Will needs Much's simple common sense.'

'But the tax collector…'

Placing a finger over his lips, Marion smiled as she stopped his sentence mid-flow. 'We will stop him before he gets to Nottingham; you, me, John, Nasir and Tuck.'

'But we don't even know which road he'll be coming in from, and he's bound to have extra guards with him this time.'

Marion agreed. 'I've been thinking about what Edward told us about Elin being a friend of the Captain of the Guard.'

'Go on.'

'It's market day in Nottingham tomorrow. Most of the traders will arrive this evening and sleep in their stalls tonight.'

'What's that got to do with anything?'

'When I was living at the castle, the captain would always lead the patrol around the city personally, on the evening of the market set-up. A "show of strength" he called it. Making sure that none of the stalls are broken into overnight.'

Robin smiled, 'You think we should go shopping and have a little talk with the captain in the morning?'

'Actually, I was going to suggest we went and gave him a hand tonight.' Reaching up on her tiptoes, Marion kissed Robin's cheek. 'I'm sure the stall holders would appreciate a little extra security.'

Robin's grin widened as he stared into her eyes. 'Did I ever tell you how much I love the colour of your eyes?'

'Many times.' She gave him another kiss, before slipping her palm back into his. 'Let's go back to the others. We need to talk to the captain. Once we've done that, I've got a plan that should—hopefully— help all of us. And that, if we're lucky, results in no one getting hurt.'

Fira had never felt so cold. Although the cloak she wore swaddled her shoulders, it did nothing to quell the chill of fear that made her body shake. She felt as if she'd never be warm again.

Glancing at Adam as he sat next to her, a scarf wrapped around his mouth to stop him from calling out the truth of their situation, a wave of guilt added itself to that she already carried on her shoulders.

It had only taken a few seconds of their incarceration for her to realise that the men holding them had nothing to do with either her uncle, Robin Hood, or any other noble outlaw. These were the men that she and Lia had fought the previous day— this was all about their humiliation and getting revenge.

I bet that horrible Welshman is behind this.

Doing her best not to inhale the damp stench that came from the swathe of material that gagged her, Fira tried to cheer herself up by imagining what her uncle would do when he got his hands on them.

And he will… he'll show them what it means to adopt the name Scarlet…

Fira had just shut her eyes, determined to rest until the moment came when she had to fight, when the guard Lia had injured crouched down in front of her, a dagger in his hand.

'Soon, the sheriff's sergeant will come to the village to rescue Adam. If you want Adam to live and your father to be freed, then this is what you must do…'

Lying on their stomachs at the edge of the wood, Will and Much could see into the village of Pipehall. The residents were grouped together at a relatively safe distance from the barn, but even from their hiding place, they could see that the villagers were nervous.

'It'll be dark in a few hours.' Much peered anxiously up at Will. 'I can't see anyone guarding the barn.'

'They're all inside. At least, that's what Pretty Lia said after she'd heard the local gossip.'

'I wish I hadn't mentioned she was pretty,' Much mumbled.

Taking no notice, Will stabbed a finger in the direction of the villagers. 'We need to get into that barn. Do you see the way that lot are looking at it?'

'They's got the look Tuck gives us if we leave any of his cooking.'

'Yeah. He hates that, he…'

A faint movement to their left saw Much grabbing Will's arm. 'Look! Chain mail—through the trees.'

Will mouthed, 'How many?'

Much held up four fingers.

Still flat on his stomach, Will shuffled forwards to try and get a better view of the scene before them.

'I'm not sure about this, Much. If it wasn't Fira we were trying to save, it'd be different—but it is, and with just two of us…'

'Three.'

The outlaws rolled over fast, just as Lia dropped to the ground beside them.

Will didn't bother to disguise his sigh of relief that it was Lia and not one of the soldiers Much had spotted. 'What the hell are you doing here?'

'Would you leave one of your friends in danger and not help?'

'No,' Much answered without hesitation.

'And you were just saying you wished you had others to help you.'

Much nodded hard. 'Yeah, you were, Will.'

'Well then,' Lia shuffled closer to Much, 'it's just as well I came back.'

Will sighed, 'You any good with that bow and arrow you're carrying?'

'As good as I am creeping up on experienced outlaws without them even noticing.'

'Point taken.' Scarlet turned back to watch the village.

Much beamed with pride. 'I'm good with a bow too. Robin says you have to be if you is gonna survive as…'

'Shush…' Will couldn't help but smile at the young man beside him, 'Alright, Much, this is hardly the time to show off to—' he checked himself, not wanting to embarrass his friend. 'Look, something's happening…'

CHAPTER EIGHT

Sergeant Sparrow rode into the village, flanked by two mounted soldiers. Determined not to show how nervous he was at the prospect of tackling outlaws (and not to mention tackling outlaws as the light of the day was beginning to fail), he was shouting before he'd even reined in his horse.

'Fira Scathlock! You will release Adam the Brewer right now, or my men will break down the barn door and drag you out!'

Dismounting and passing his horse to a startled villager, Sparrow shrieked towards the door for a second time. 'You have until the count of three to obey. If you and your men do not come out then you will hang alongside your father. Tomorrow!'

From the safety of the trees, Will tensed as he and Much witnessed the drama unfolding before them.

Much nudged his friend. 'He just said he were going to hang your brother tomorrow.'

'I 'eard him.'

'I wish the others…' Much let the words trail into the air as he felt, rather than heard, the heavy sigh that escaped Scarlet's lips.

'I wish the others were here too, but they ain't, so we are just going to have to sort this without them.' Will went back to surveying the scene before them. 'No sign of the tax man. The coward must have gone on to Nottingham and left Sparrow to do his dirty work for 'im. Figures.'

Lia whispered, 'There's no sign of the soldiers Much spotted just before I dropped in to join you. I reckon they've double backed to the other side of the village.'

Much muttered to Scarlet, 'They won't have gone far, will they.'

'No, they won't.' With a derisive snort he rocked back onto his knees. 'You both ready?'

'Yeah,' Lia replied, while Much nodded, his gaze never leaving the activity by the barn.

'Good.' Scarlet drew his sword. 'You two, aim for the guards—suppose we'd better leave Sparrow alive. When the guards are down Lia, you run back to the inn. Fast.'

'No way!' Lia notched an arrow to her bow. 'Fira is my friend, I'm going to…'

Much reached out a hand to her, before thinking better of it and withdrawing it to fix an arrow to his bow. 'Lia, you *must* go to the inn. If Sparrow hears you weren't in the tavern this evening, while this was happening, he might start to suspect you too.'

'But I'm known to be Fira's friend, so he's bound to suspect me anyway.'

'Possibly, but he don't know it was you for sure. Please,' Much coaxed, 'it's safest for you to be far away from here. For you *and* for Fira. I promise.'

Lia grumbled, 'Right.'

Will grumbled impatiently, 'I thought you two said you were ready!'

As Much and Lia pulled back their bows, each focusing on one of the guards either side of Sparrow, Will held up his hand. 'Alright then, on my mark…'

'Fira Scathlock! I'm going to count to three, if you haven't come out by then, my men will come in!' Sparrow loudly addressed the closed barn doors. 'One… Two…' He hesitated, listening for any sign of movement from within the barn. When none came, he added, 'Your time is running out, Scathlock woman!'

A stillness fell over Pipehall as everyone held their breath.

As the seconds ticked by, the guards drew their swords, and Sparrow roared, 'Three!'

Men, women and children scattered, their cries of alarm and confusion mingling with the unexpected hum of arrows flying across the village. Sparrow and his men didn't have time to register that they were under attack until two of them hit the ground, arrows protruding from their backs.

Sparrow dived for cover as, twisting round in panic, he saw Will Scarlet and Much the Miller's Son, swords drawn, running in his direction.

Backing his way towards the barn door, Sparrow called out to Elin's associates within. 'Robin Hood's men! That cursed Scarlet is here!'

Diving forwards, Will grabbed Sparrow by the scruff of the neck. 'That's not a very nice way to greet an old friend, is it.'

'Friend?'

'Enemy, then—almost the same thing.'

Wriggling to try and escape the outlaw's grasp, every trace of bravado gone, the harassed sergeant spluttered, 'How did you get here so fast?'

'Borrowed some horses.'

Sparrow's eyes shone with fear as he yelled out, 'He's got me! Will Scarlet's got me!'

A second later, the barn doors flew open, and Simon ran out, brandishing his sword. 'Where's your respect? Don't you know that's the sheriff's man. Let go of him!'

'My pleasure.' Will threw Sparrow so hard at Simon that their heads knocked together with a stomach-churning clunk.

'Arrgghhh...' Sparrow's knees buckled as he cradled his forehead in both hands. By the time he was on his feet again, Simon had already recovered himself and was locked in a sword fight. A fight which was over almost before it had begun, as Scarlet disarmed and winded his adversary in three easy moves.

Much, already fighting James, almost lost his

footing when a woman came running out of the barn, her sword aloft. One look at the determined, incredibly angry, expression on her face told him—in no uncertain terms—that this was Will Scarlet's niece.

A furious Fira, sword at the ready, jumped in front of the fallen, wounded, Simon, and attacked her uncle.

Finding himself having to use more effort and concentration to block Fira's blows than he would ever have had admitted to, Will spoke through gritted teeth. 'What the hell are you doing, girl?'

'Protecting myself against the likes of you!' Fira shouted back, making sure everyone around her could hear.

A wheezing Simon scurried to his feet, and joined James in fighting Much, as Will bawled, 'Much! Hurry up with those guards and free the brewer!'

Battling as hard as he could, Much increased the rate of his sword thrusts. 'I'm trying my best, but there are two of them and only one of me!'

Suddenly, an arrow flew out from between the trees and James sank to the muddy ground with a cry of pain.

With a rueful grin, and a private thank you to Lia for disobeying them and staying in the woods after all, Much called to Scarlet, 'Make that one of them!'

As Fira continued to fight her uncle, she spoke with quiet urgency. 'Adam's hogtied in there.'

'What did he ever do to you!?'

'Nothing! He's my friend.' Fira pleaded with her eyes, hoping he'd pick up on her urgency. 'You *must* lose the fight. Please, Uncle Will... please...'

Keeping up his carefully placed onslaught, so he could hold his own while making sure he didn't actually injure his niece, Will muttered, 'Why? What's going on?'

'I'll explain later on.'

'Alright, later it is, but... Hang on, where's that coward, Sparrow?'

Fira kept up her rally of blows. 'Run away, I reckon.'

'Then we can stop fighting... there's no one here too—' Will was about to lower his guard when he heard the faint pounding of horses' hooves and the roll of wagon wheels approaching announced that there were more pressing issues to worry about. 'Much! There's more soldiers coming! Those four you spotted in the woods! Get the brewer!'

With a desperate lunge, Much ducked down, then lifted his sword upwards and outwards, thrusting it into Simon's side, before he sprinted to the barn.

'Hurry, Much!' Will kept one eye on the barn door while fighting Fira, only to exhale with a puff of relief as he saw his friend and Adam rush outside.

'Got him, Will!'

'Get him to safety! Go! And grab Pretty Lia on the way.'

Much hesitated as he saw Will still locked in a battle with Fira. 'But what about…'

'Get out of here, Much! Now!'

As the wagon they'd heard coming, arrived in the village, Much grabbed Adam's arm and ran towards the wood.

'I'm so sorry, Uncle Will, but this is the only way to save my father,' Fira spoke fast as they fought closer together. 'There'll be more soldiers in that wagon. I *need* to overcome you, Uncle! I *must!*'

'Well, bloody well get on with it then!'

CHAPTER NINE

'Your friend has not arrived, Captain.'

The sheriff's earlier good humour had steadily slipped away with each hour that had passed, and the king's taxes had not been delivered.

'Elin will come, my lord.'

'I admire your confidence, Captain, but I do not share it.'

'As soon as I have overseen the setting up of the market, I will be riding to the Derby Road with my men, my lord.' The captain placed his helmet upon his head.

The sheriff's eyes narrowed. 'You think he will still come so late in the day?'

'Normally, I would think it unlikely, but Nottingham is awash with rumour that Will Scarlet's brother has been captured in Lichfield—the place from which Elin has headed, so…'

'Captured!?' De Rainault was on his feet. 'Scarlet's kin! Why wasn't I told about this?'

'Because I didn't want to disappoint you, my lord. If Scarlet goes to try and rescue his brother…'

'Then he could be captured as well!'

'Indeed, my lord,' The captain smiled, 'If that has happened, then it would explain a delay in Elin's appearance, for surely he'd wish to see one of the men who already robbed him twice, arrested.'

Sitting down again, the sheriff raised a goblet to his lips. 'That would make sense.'

'May I leave, my lord?'

'You may.' As the captain bowed and made to leave, De Rainault called after him. 'I still want to see Elin the Welshman in this hall by midnight—and if Will Scarlet isn't in custody, I will want to know why!'

Nasir crept back to where John and Robin were hidden at the far side of the market.

'Two soldiers with him.'

Robin readied his bow. 'John, tell Marion and Tuck.'

Moving without a sound, Little John slipped into the empty tavern. 'He's coming. Get ready.'

As John went back to Robin and Nasir, Tuck muttered, 'I still think that the captain will be suspicious by how quiet the tavern is. Normally, there would be people coming in and out. It's a noisy place... or it was before we paid Joseph the innkeeper more than he'd make in one evening, just to borrow the place for an hour!'

Marion, who'd admitted it was the weakest part of her plan, couldn't argue. 'We'll make it work, Tuck.'

'Alright, Little Flower.' Tuck stood ready on one side of the open tavern door, while Marion stood on the other, a rope in her hand. 'I wonder where Joseph has taken his customers?'

'No idea, but he said something about the cooper helping, so maybe, they're all in his workshop.'

Tuck was still visualising Nottingham's drinkers gathered around a load of barrels, supping from a handful of tankards and ale jugs, when he heard the swipe of a knife flying through the air. It was followed by a soft thwack, as Nasir's first victim fell from his saddle. This was rapidly followed by the whinny of a distressed horse and the fly and 'thunk' of an arrow leaving the bow and hitting its target.

Marion tensed as she waited for the inevitable cry for help from the captain, but all she caught was a curtailed, 'Wolfsh…' as the second half of the insult was muffled behind one of Little John's large palms. She knew Robin and John would be dragging the Captain of the Guard from his horse, while Nasir calmed the three horses.

My plan's working so far. Thank goodness…

'Ready?' Tuck mouthed as they heard footsteps coming their way.

Pushing her shoulders back, rope at the ready, Marion leapt into action as the furious, struggling soldier was manhandled into the tavern.

As she secured the captain's wrists behind his back, Tuck knotted a gag between his teeth. Then, while Nasir guarded the doorway, Marion watched as John pushed their prisoner onto the nearest bench, standing guard behind him while Robin, his trusty sword Albion in his hand, explained the situation.

'We hear that you know Elin the Welshman. That he's a friend. Is that true? Just nod or shake your head.'

His eyes gleaming with hatred, the captain gave a reluctant nod.

'Good,' Robin went on. 'He is due in Sherwood with the tax money soon. Is he coming in by the Newark Road?'

Before the captain could indicate his response, John grabbed hold of his hair and slowly pulled his head back. 'Don't even think about lying to us. That sort of behaviour has consequences. We know that if the sheriff is expecting Elin, *you'll* know about it. Yes?'

The captain nodded again.

'So,' Robin asked again. 'The Newark Road?'

The captain shook his head.

'The bridge at Aldbury?'

Another shake of the head.

'Derby Road?'

This time there was no reaction.

'Ah…' Robin tapped Albion's blade against the soldier's high cheekbone. 'Derby Road, at the turn towards Nottingham?'

This time the captain gave a tiny nod.

'There, that didn't hurt, did it?' John ruffled the man's hair. 'Now all we need to know is when the sheriff is expecting him.'

Robin asked, 'The day after tomorrow?'

This time the captain shook his head at once.

'Tomorrow?'

Again, their captive shook his head.

Robin looked up at John, who took a handful of the captain's hair again, asking, 'In three days' time?'

Hurried, muted words rained into the gag, as the captain struggled to speak.

'Alright, John, let go.' As the captain rocked forward, cursing into the scarf between his teeth, Robin asked, 'Tonight?'

The captain gave a slight inclination of his head.

'Tonight, on the Derby Road,' Robin spoke fast as he exchanged an urgent glance with John. 'Thank you, Captain. I'm glad it's so soon. That means De Rainault won't get too mad with you for having time off.'

Until that moment the captain had looked angry. Now, he looked afraid.

'Don't panic, Captain,' Marion smiled, 'I'm sure the sheriff be more forgiving than he would have been if you'd had two or three days away from your post.'

Robin levered the captain back to his feet. 'We are going to untie you now. Then you are going to go to Nasir, who will accompany you, on your horse, for a little ride into Sherwood. To the Derby Road, to be exact.'

Protesting under the muffle in his mouth, the

captain attempted to free his wrists, but a single warning glare from the Saracen put a stop to that.

'Don't worry, Captain, we'll take good care of you.' Friar Tuck gave the soldier a hearty whack on the back. 'Anyway, Sherwood is lovely this time of year. You can have a night off in the great outdoors.'

John grinned, 'And you can help us get the people's money back from your friend, Elin. That'll be nice, won't it?'

Leaving the captain for a moment, Robin gestured for his friends to come closer. He spoke fast. 'If Elin is due tonight, we don't have much time.'

'We could have already missed him,' Nasir hissed.

Not arguing with this possibility, Robin said, 'Hopefully we haven't—we'll go now. But we'll travel along the road from Nottingham to the junction with Derby Road—if we have missed him, then he'll have to go that way towards the castle, so there's still a chance we could intercept him.'

'Aye,' John agreed. 'He'd never travel through Sherwood anyway, especially this early in the morning.'

'It's four miles, so we'll need to take all of the horses you tethered up Nasir, not just the captain's.'

Robin turned to Tuck. 'Stay here, square things with Joseph the innkeeper, and makes sure this place is full of its usual drinkers before the rest of the sheriff's guards notice how quiet it is. Reassure Joseph too. If he gets any trouble from the sheriff or Gisburne, we'll put things right. Then, head to the camp as fast as you can—we're going to have a lot of money to count out very soon.'

Moving fast, Little John hauled the captain up onto his horse, in front of Nasir. Robin mounted one of the other soldiers' horses. He reached out a hand for Marion, who leapt up beside him, just as John jumped into the third saddle.

They were cantering through the forest before Marion spoke. 'What was that all about with John? Him yanking the captain's hair like that. He was acting just like Will does.'

'I don't know.' Robin kept his eyes on the track ahead, adjusting the reins to guide the horse through Sherwood. 'Maybe he was channelling his inner Scarlet.'

CHAPTER TEN

Elin the Welshman was regretting his decision not to delay his trip to Nottingham until daybreak. At the time, it had felt sensible not to keep the Sheriff of Nottingham waiting for the tax money—especially as he'd lost the last two consignments. But now, as nighttime took over from the evening, and the shadows cast by the trees of Sherwood became longer and more threatening, he was having serious second thoughts.

'Suffering the sharp end of De Rainault's temper would be better than this,' Elin muttered as he urged his horse on, breaking from a hasty walk into a trot.

Bouncing against the hard wooden seat, he felt every bump in the road as a cold sweat broke out across his shoulder blades.

*If I'd waited until the Scathlock Woman was taken,
then Simon and James could have come with me...*

He shot a nervous stare into the forest to his
left, before immediately feeling that he was being
watched from the right and twisted his neck round
to look in that direction instead.

He blew out a puff of air, watching as it frosted
in front of him.

*The sheriff would have been cross if I was late...
but not as cross as he'll be if I lose the money for a third
time.*

Elin tried to halt his spiralling fears, as he
desperately searched ahead of himself; half hoping
to see help in the form of an escort from the castle,
and half dreading seeing anyone at all.

*The sheriff's probably already angry. There's not
much of today left to deliver the taxes in.*

Swallowing against his dry throat, Elin urged his
horse onwards as he tried to reassure himself.

'As soon as Sparrow has Scarlet and his accursed
family under lock and key, De Rainault will forgive
me for falling foul of the outlaws those two times
before... and I know they won't expect me to come
to Sherwood at night, so I'll be alright.' He glimpsed
into the trees again.

There's no one there. I'm imagining things.

Elin forced himself to stop peering into the forest and concentrate on the road ahead, and the meal he'd share with the Captain of the Guard when he reached the castle.

However hard he tried, however, he couldn't shift the echo of Sergeant Sparrow's words, '...*every outlaw I've ever had the misfortune to meet had been perfectly at home in the dark...*'.

'Talk. Now!'

Will stared at his niece, as they were bounced along inside a prison wagon, on the way back to Lichfield.

Glancing anxiously at the two guards that accompanied them, Fira was sulky. 'I wanted to help people. I wanted to...'

Biting his tongue, Scarlet said, 'I get that—believe me, I do. But I need to know what's been going on. Why were you and the brewer in the barn with those poor excuses for swordsmen?'

'I don't know where to start.'

Will's patience shattered and he barked, 'Try!'

Fira fired back, 'Don't shout at me like that!

I just told you that I was trying to help. Like *you* do!'

'Like me? Hell's teeth, Fira! I ain't got no choice! What other path is there for me? But you—you've got a home and food and friends and...'

'And total boredom!'

Niece and uncle glared at each from either side of the wagon, where they were sat, hands bound, with silent guards to their sides. The feel of the rumble of the wheels beneath them changed, as the route they were taking merged from soft grass to hard trackway.

Fira shuddered. 'I reckon we're almost in Lichfield.'

'I bet we're being taken to where your father is. The town gaol.' Will turned to the guard next to him. 'Well, soldier boy—are we?'

The guard stared at him, but said nothing.

'Not chatty, the soldiers around here, are they?' Will rolled his eyes. 'And there I was, planning to ask 'em to read me a bedtime story before they tucked us up in the gaol all snug-like.'

'Bet they can't read anyway.' Fira threw the nearest guard a hateful glare as she tried to manoeuvre her wrists, but they were bound too tightly. 'Maybe they've got nothing worth saying.'

Understanding his niece's frustration, Will tried to calm down. 'Why did you have to fight me?'

The wagon slowed to a stop and Fira gave a sideways glance at the guards. 'How about I answer that question later as well?'

'After we've laid out these guards, you mean.'

'Yeah.'

Swinging round, Fira and Will punched both guards hard in the face, laying them out before either of them had cottoned on to what was about to happen.

'Skilled blow. Well done.' Will regarded Fira with respect. 'Now, talk. Tell me everything. Fast. Before the wagon comes to a full stop.'

'I've been trying to do good—and *they* made *me* look like a kidnapper! Told me—and everyone else nearby—that they were my men. I didn't take Adam hostage, they did! Them two you and Much fought; they ain't nothing to do with me.'

'Lia told us that,' Will grinned. 'And then she underlined the point by shooting one of 'em.'

'She's a good shot.' Fira's brief smile fractured as she thought back to her time in the barn. 'They tried to convince me that they'd come from you— that they were Robin Hood's men too, and you had persuaded Robin to send them to help me.'

'Cunning…'

'For a few minutes, I thought maybe they were telling the truth.' Fira's cheeks burned almost the same colour as her hair as she confessed. 'I wanted it to be true. Because, if it had been, then no one who didn't deserve to be hurt would suffer.'

'We do try not to hurt too many people.' Feeling his conscience nudging him, Will added, 'Robin gets cross otherwise.'

'They tied Adam up—and then me. You'd never do that.'

Will's expression darkened as he said, 'Go on, girl, tell me the rest, we're running out of time.'

'Sparrow and his men couldn't care less about what I did—or had tried to do to Elin. All they wanted was an excuse to capture you! If I didn't do what the men in the barn with me and Adam said, Sparrow would kill my father. Or get the sheriff's men to do it for him.'

Will nodded as the wagon slowed further.

'Uncle Will, where's Lia now? Is she alright?'

98

Much and Lia kept close together as they edged through an amassing crowd outside the sheriff's sergeant's office.

'What's everyone doing out here?'

Lia grunted. 'Welcome to Lichfield, Much—the place where everyone loves a show! The entire town will know what's happened by now. Shame we had to close the tavern; they'll be missing having a drink while they wait to be entertained by whatever's going to happen next.'

'I remember what the townsfolk are like from when we was here before.'

'You've been here before, Much?'

'I'll tell you 'bout it when we're all safe.'

Lia went a little pink. 'Will you? That'd be nice.'

Noting Lia's wistful air, Much mumbled, 'Oh yeah, right—so then, yes. I...' Pulling himself together, he refocused on the action outside. 'We must stay out of sight.'

Checking left and right, Lia grabbed his hand. 'Quick—in here.'

They darted into the nearest building, as the sound of a wagon approaching sent the crowd outside into an expectant silence.

'This is the dyer's house. If I know him and his wife, they'll be right at the heart of the action, waiting to see what happens to Scathlock, so this place will be empty.' Taking the lead, Lia clambered up two stairs at a time. 'If my guess is right, there'll be a good view from here, we should be able to—'

'Shh…' Much bobbed down as they reached the unshuttered window. '…Look, Sparrow is riding next to the cart and there are two other guards plus the driver.'

'They'll be guards inside with Will and Fira too, I expect.'

Much smiled. 'I don't think we'll have to worry about them. Are you ready?'

'Always.' Lia took an arrow from her quiver and notched it onto her bowstring.

CHAPTER ELEVEN

'We shouldn't have left Tuck behind,' Robin muttered as they waited beneath the trees that marked the turn from Derby Road towards Nottingham. 'We're already short-handed because of Will and Much.'

Marion watched the road ahead. 'If you hadn't, and someone had noticed the inn was closed, even if it was just for a while, then Joseph would have gotten into trouble, and you'd never have forgiven yourself.'

'I know.'

'Well then.' Marion tensed as the faint sound of a cart rumbling in their direction made them both reach into their quivers for an arrow. 'Do you think the captain told us the truth about Elin travelling alone?'

'No.' Robin let his gaze stray from the road into the trees on either side of the road, as if he was expecting to see a hoard of soldiers appear at any moment.

On the opposite side of the road, John and Nasir had heard the cart too. John grabbed the captain by his cloak and hoisted him to his feet. 'Do you understand what you have to do?'

Still bound and gagged, the captain nodded.

Nasir stepped nearer to their prisoner. 'You do this, then no blood will be spilt.'

John pushed his face up against the frightened captain's, 'But, if you let us down, there *will* be blood spilt—and it'll be yours.'

The captain glared up at the outlaw, and nodded again, hating that he couldn't speak his mind, but common sense telling him it was probably just as well he had the gag in at that moment.

'If you let Elin see what's happening at the back of his cart before we're done, then you won't live to discover the consequences because Robin will have an arrow ready to hit you square in the back. Yes?' John didn't see the bound man nod again; he'd already resumed his vigil, waiting for the cart he could hear to come into view.

The sheriff glared at the plate before him.

'Pork! Again.'

The servant who'd delivered his supper had already bobbed a curtsey and made a hasty exit, fully aware how displeased her master would be with the evening's fare.

'So much for the captain having a word with the cook.' He stabbed a slice of meat with his knife. 'I should have been suspicious when he said he was friends with the man. Who bothers making friends with servants?'

Dropping the knife, the meat still attached, back to the platter, the sheriff watched the flames in the fireplace dance before him. 'And there's still no sign of the taxes... If that Welshman lets me down again, then he *and* his *friend,* the captain, had better look out...'

The Welshman sharply tugged the reins to bring the horse to an abrupt stop. He blinked away the sweat that ran into his eyes, unsure if he was really seeing the figure that had just emerged from the trees to his left.

It took Elin a moment to realise that not only did he know the man who was shuffling in tiny steps towards the cart, but also that he was gagged, and his arms were bound behind his back. Not just that, but that the man's movements were further restricted by a rope that tied his legs together, just above the knees.

Tightening his grip on the leather reins, Elin froze; torn between jumping down to help his friend and staying where he was as his brain screamed, *it's a trap.*

As the Captain of the Guard tottered clumsily towards him, Elin could see the desperate gleam in his eyes. The captain had reached his horse before the Welshman could hear the muffled pleading.

'Elin… help me…'

With another careful look around him, and seeing nothing more than the leaves on the branches swaying in the breeze of the chilly night, Elin took a deep breath. As much as he didn't want to explain to the sheriff why he'd lost the tax money again, he also didn't want to tell him that he'd failed to free his most senior solider—and that was even before

Elin's consideration that the bound man before him was his friend.

Coming to a split second decision, Elin jumped down from the cart. Keeping hold of the reins, he hurried to his friend's side and tugged down the gag.

Coughing and spluttering, the captain made a guttural throaty sound as he worked enough moisture into his mouth to be able to speak.

'What happened?' Elin knelt to untie the ropes at his friend's knees.

'Hood,' The captain spoke softly, his mind picturing the arrival of an arrow in his back at any minute.

'He captured you?'

'Escaped… sort of.' The captain flexed out one leg at a time as the ropes at his knees fell to the floor.

Elin shot another glance into the forest. 'He's nearby?'

'No,' The captain gulped, forcing himself not to react when he saw the stealthy figure of Nasir making his way to the back of the cart. 'They are waiting for you by the old stone bridge at Aldbury.'

'Thank goodness,' Elin blew out a sigh of relief, before a crease formed on his already furrowed brow. 'How did you get all the way over here?'

'Very slowly.' A fresh trickle of fear ran up his spine as the captain willed Elin to believe him. 'They've been there all day expecting you to arrive.'

'How did you escape?' Elin set to work on freeing his friend's hands.

'They left me in the forest near to where they were waiting. I stole away. I was sure they wouldn't follow and risk missing you arrive.'

Elin nodded. What he was hearing made sense. 'Especially as they are two men down.'

'Scarlet and the halfwit boy?' The captain stretched his arms out to the sides to loosen the muscles. 'Does that mean the rumours are true, and the innkeeper has been arrested?'

'They are. It was my idea,' Elin said smugly, 'I knew Scarlet would try and save him. It was just a bonus that the boy went with him. They're in Lichfield. Sparrow should have them locked in the local gaol by now.'

'Is that so? Well, that's cheered me up a bit.'

'When the sheriff gets the taxes he'll be happy too—especially if we can tell him that two of Hood's men are taken,' Elin smiled. 'Come on, I'll give you a lift to the castle. It'll be good to have company, and it'll be a nicer trip now I know that I'm not going to be intercepted by outlaws.'

Seeing Marion move, ghostlike, from the cart to the forest, her arms full of bags of coin, the captain put his hand out to Elin to stop him returning to the cart.

'I just need a minute.' Holding onto his friend, the captain bent his legs at the knee, one at a time. 'I've been bound for ages.'

'Bet you're hungry too. I've got some bread in the cart.' Elin went to turn, but again the captain stopped him, just as Nasir ran back into Sherwood, his arms full of money bags as well. 'Wait.'

'Wait?' Elin frowned, 'I can't wait too long, if I don't get to the sheriff before midnight…'

The sight of Marion waving to him, before she disappeared into the trees, made the captain sag with relief.

'Are you alright, my friend?' Elin but his arm around the captain's shoulders. 'You aren't wounded as well, are you?'

'Not yet.' The captain stood upright, his voice still subdued, but less croaky. 'Hood's men tied me up and humiliated me, but it is the sheriff who'll probably hurt me. At the very least, I can wave goodbye to the promotion…'

'Promotion?'

'And if the cook has given him pork, I've no

hope…' The captain muttered, confusing the taxman further.

'What are you talking about? It's not your fault Hood caught you, and the taxes are safe, so…'

Elin's face drained of colour as the captain slowly shook his head from side to side. The Welshman spoke quietly, as if not quite daring to utter the words. 'They took the money whilst we were talking, didn't they.'

'They did. A bloodless heist they called it. Had the cheek to tell me I should learn from their example—that it wasn't always necessary to hurt people to get what I wanted. But, there was an arrow targeted on my back, nonetheless.'

Elin gulped.

'The sheriff is going to kill us—literally.' The captain stared into the empty cart.

'What are we going to do?' Elin's Welsh lilt chimed with fear.

'I wish I knew.' The captain rubbed a hand over his bruised wrists. 'I really wish I knew.'

CHAPTER TWELVE

The wagon and horses slowed as it drove through the jeering townsfolk.

Jumping from his horse, Sparrow hollered haughtily, 'Move aside! Move aside... Make way for the prisoners...' Gesturing to the building that combined his office and the town gaol, he waved his sword around aimlessly. 'Throw the prisoners in with their kin!'

As the prison wagon's door was opened, Will and Fira leapt out, knocking the guard to the ground in the process, provoking a cheer of approval from the ever-obliging crowd.

The blood drained from Sparrow's face as his moment of triumph began to disintegrate before his eyes. He screeched, 'Stop them! They're—'

'We're what, Sergeant?' Running forward, Will lifted his tethered hands and threw his arms around Sparrow, trapping him against his chest. With deft skill, Scarlet squeezed his captive's torso, pinning his arms to his sides, just as an arrow flew through the air, hitting the side of the wagon, only inches from where they stood.

'Ahhh! An arrow! The other outlaws must be here too!'

Another arrow crossed the square, hitting James square in the shin. He howled in agony and anger, buckling at the knees, before landing on the well-trodden muddy earth. 'My leg! You…'

'Oh, do shut up!' Fira spat at his pained, crumpled expression. 'You wanted my uncle to come here so you could capture him, didn't you!' Drawing back her tethered arms, she punched James hard in the face with both her fists. 'That's for scaring Adam!' Then she kicked him. 'And that's for scaring me!'

Sparrow, still trapped between Will's arms, watched in terror, as his guard writhed on the ground.

'Bit of advice for you, Sergeant Sparrow,' Will growled, 'Always tie your prisoners hands *behind* their backs, because if you tie them in front…' Will paused as Fira punched a second guard with such

110

force that he staggered to the side, blood pouring from his nose. '...then we can still hurt people.'

Not daring to speak, Sparrow simply gulped.

Observing his niece with pride, Will tightened his arms around Sparrow. 'You must tell me where you learnt to punch like that, Fira.'

'Watched you when I was a little girl, didn't I.'

'Oh, I...'

But Fira wasn't listening. She was confronting the nearest member of the watching crowd. 'Untie me. Now—or I'll tell my uncle that you refused to help me.'

The town's dyer worked fast, bitter experience telling him that was no empty threat. Ignoring the jibes of the people around him, he did exactly as he was told.

Will laughed as he watched Fira at work, but soon regretted letting his concentration slip, for Sparrow swung an elbow back to wind Will in the stomach, crouched low, and was suddenly free of Will's tethered grip.

Acting on unusually swift instincts, he then grabbed a sword from a nearby soldier and swiped it upwards at a reeling Will.

Fira yelled, 'Watch out, uncle!'

As Will shot backwards, his own wrists still

111

hampered by ropes, Fira pulled a knife from her boot. 'Duck!'

The blade sliced through the air, landing in the top of Sparrow's arm with a sickening thump. Dropping the sword to the ground, he screamed. 'My arm! There's a knife in my arm!'

'Well spotted.' Scarlet kicked the sheriff's sergeant in the knee. 'If you don't free my brother, your arm will be the least of your worries!'

'But he is guilty of—'

'He is guilty of *nothing!*' Fira snarled at a deathly-pale Sparrow, as she retrieved her knife from his flesh, wiping the sergeant's blood on his tunic before cutting through her uncle's restraints. 'You just wanted to lure Will Scarlet here so you could imprison him! You used *me* as an excuse—a trap! All so you could get back into the sheriff's good books!'

Sparrow spluttered, 'I... errr...' as Will grabbed him around the neck.

Fira spoke directly into the terrified sergeant's ear. 'You should be careful what you wish for! I'm sure the Sheriff of Nottingham would be delighted to hear how you failed to catch two outlaws, arrested an innocent man, and tried to frame his daughter!'

'But, you! You're guilty—you were seen. You—'

'Do I really have to choke you?' Will placed his palm at Sparrow's throat.

Shaking his head fast, Sparrow gave a splutter of relief as Scarlet let go of him. 'How dare you take the word of that crooked Welshman over my niece!' he hissed, 'A coward of a taxman who disappeared before the fighting started!'

Sparrow tried to reply but it came out as a throaty stammer, so Scarlet continued on, 'Fira Scathlock is guilty of nothing more than trying to help her fellow man. You should try it sometime; it leaves a nice warm glow in the heart.'

'But... she—' Sparrow managed.

'Did absolutely nothing *at all.*' Will's eyes blazed. 'Do you understand me, Sparrow?'

Sparrow nodded over-eagerly, 'Uh-huh.'

'Good. Now, I think you should release my brother—the people of Lichfield appear to be thirsty.'

A cheer went up from the crowd as Scarlet deposited Sparrow in an unceremonious heap upon the road.

With a hand at his bruised neck, Sparrow almost tripped over his own feet in his rush to get away from the outlaw. Will called after the sergeant, 'If you know what's good for you, I'd leave trying to catch Robin Hood to the sheriff.'

'I will. And that Gisbeard!'

'Gisbuuuurne!' Will shouted, as Sparrow disappeared from view, in a desperate hurry to get to the gaol and release the purveyor of the finest ale in Lichfield.

CHAPTER THIRTEEN

'Well done, Little Flower, that was a good plan.'

Sinking down next to where Tuck was sorting a mound of coins into piles of ten, Marion stretched her legs out towards the fire. 'I'm just glad it worked.'

'I'd say it worked a treat.' Robin picked up a bag of coins and weighed it in his palm with satisfaction. 'And without a single soldier having to suffer either.'

Nasir ran a cleaning rag over the blade of his knife. 'The captain will be sore for a few days, I think.'

'Good,' John grimaced. As the other outlaws exchanged knowing glances, John scrubbed a hand through his beard. 'What is it?'

Robin passed Tuck a pile of money purses as he said, 'I think we need Scarlet to get back.'

'Well, of course we do, Robin!'

Marion chuckled, 'Temper, temper, John.'

'I'm not cross, lass, I'm just…'

'You grabbed the Captain of the Guard by the hair and tugged his head right back.' Robin threw a nearby twig onto the fire. 'And now you're getting narky with me.'

With a slow smile, Nasir added, 'In the forest, you told him that if he let us down, he would not live.'

'So what?'

'So what?' Marion's smile widened, 'When did you start saying, "so what" John Little? That's the sort of thing that…'

'That Scarlet says!' John's jaw dropped open as he sank down, kneeling close to the warmth of the fire. 'I've gone all Will Scarlet!'

'You have.' Robin passed his friend a flask of ale. 'I don't think this group needs more than one hothead, do you?'

Taking a drink, Little John shook his not-so-hot-head, as he thought back to his recent behaviour. 'I didn't think I had it in me!'

Tuck counted ten coins into a pile, 'Sounds like it worked, though. You got the captain to do what we wanted.'

'It *did* work,' Nasir agreed.

John chuckled. 'Who'd have thought it. Just for a moment there I was John Scarlet.'

Marion smiled. 'I can just imagine what Much would say if he was here.'

'What's that, Little Flower?'

'He'd say, if you were John Scarlet, then Scarlet would be Little Will.'

John laughed, 'I don't think we need three guesses to imagine what Will would say to that!'

Marion poured ten coins into the next purse, her smile dimming. 'I hope Will and Much are alright.'

'I'm sure they are.' Robin looked at the money that they'd soon be taking back to the villagers of Nottinghamshire. 'But tomorrow, we'll head through Sherwood on the Lichfield road, just in case.'

Sat with his back against a thick trunk, Will rested his legs out in front of him. Looking up at the canopy of the trees, he could see the moon casting its glow across Pipehall Wood. Much was perched next to him, an expression of contentment on his

117

face, while Lia and Fira both gave the impression that they were waiting to be told off.

However, when Will did speak, his voice was gentle. 'How long have you been carrying a knife in your boot, Fira?'

'Years—you never know when trouble will strike. The inn can get a bit rowdy sometimes. The unexpected arrival of a knife into a conversation when a guest has had too much beer—and unacceptable ideas—can give a girl the edge.'

Will grunted with amusement as he pictured the scene his niece was creating. 'You used your knife well today. I was impressed.'

'Thanks, Uncle Will.'

Unhooking the water pouch from his belt, Much took a swig. 'What will you two do now?'

Will surprised everyone by saying, 'You could come with us? Both of you. Robin wouldn't turn away such good bow and knife skills.'

'Wow… that would be…' Fira only just stopped herself accepting the invitation. 'Thank you, that means a lot to me—to us—that you think we're good enough to come with you, but no. Sherwood is already well protected. There are many other places that need the sort of help you give.'

Lia tucked her knees up under her chin as she

turned to look at her friend. 'I agree, but we can't stay here. Sergeant Sparrow will never stop watching you now, Fira. As soon as you put one foot out of line, he'll arrest you out of spite.'

Will was about to agree with Lia, when Fira said, 'There are rumours of an unscrupulous landlord abusing his workers near Tamworth. We'll go there to start with—after that, who knows?'

Taking his knife from his belt, Will scored the tip into the ground next to him, a sign that told Much his friend was worried but wasn't going to admit it. 'You'll move from trouble to trouble?'

'There are worse ways to live, Uncle.'

'There are.' Will got to his feet. 'Do you have a message you want me to give your father before I leave Lichfield?'

Fira swallowed as she understood what her uncle was saying. She couldn't go back—not now. Not even to fetch some more clothes. Maybe not ever.

'Tell him I… I'll miss him and that the dyer's daughter would make a good barmaid. She's a hard worker and hates working for her parents.'

Seeing, in that moment, just how like him Fira was, Scarlet's heart went out to her. *Don't worry my girl, I'll make sure your father knows you love him.*

'And what about you, Lia?' Much asked. 'Any messages from you?'

'Thank you, but no. I've no family. It's always just been me and Fira since… well, for a very long time.'

'Alright.' Much shuffled his feet awkwardly, not quite able to make eye contact with the pretty girl with the long brown pigtail. 'You take care. Both of you.'

Opening his arms to Fira, who immediately accepted his hug, Will whispered, 'We should go.'

After a few seconds, Fira reluctantly stepped out from the safety of her uncle's arms. 'Thank you for saving my father. Both of you. For coming so far to help.'

Will shrugged. 'He's my brother.'

'Anyway, you two did most of the saving,' Much said. 'We just helped.'

Lia looked shyly at Much. 'You never did tell me about your last visit to Lichfield.'

'Maybe next time we meet.'

'Maybe…' Lia smiled as Much picked up his bow, slinging it over his shoulder, ready to depart.

'Good luck, then.' Will Scarlet regarded his niece with pride. 'Fira, do try and keep out of trouble when you can.'

Fira laughed, 'Like *you* do, you mean?'
'Yeah, my girl, just like I do.'

EPILOGUE

Will let out a hearty belch as they reached the edge of Sherwood Forest.

Much took a swig of ale from the pouch he carried. 'Nice of your brother to give us so much ale for the journey.'

'Yeah.' Will wiped the back of his hand over his mouth.

'You took long enough fetching it, though. I was beginning to wonder where...' Much broke off as realisation dawned. 'You went to see your boot seller lady, didn't you?'

Will chuckled. 'Might have popped in, just to be friendly.'

'To be friendly? Yeah right.'

'I wanted to see if she still had me old boots.'

Returning Will's ale-fuelled grin, Much asked, 'And did she?'

'Forgot to ask.'

Much laughed as he led them into familiar territory. 'Easy to be forgetful when you've drunk too much ale.'

When Will didn't reply, Much glanced back at his friend, only to see that his good humour had been replaced by a thoughtful expression. After letting a preoccupied hush lie between them for a few minutes, Much ventured, 'It's nice to be back in Sherwood again.'

'Much…' Will stopped walking as he uncharacteristically decided to share what was on his mind. '…wouldn't you have liked to go with them? With Fira and Lia? She liked you, Pretty Lia, I mean. You could have been with someone… had someone to call your own, and… maybe a wife… a family and—'

Holding up a hand to pause that thought, Much experienced a stab of the particular type of sadness that he shared with Will. 'She was nice, Lia, but she wasn't Kate.' He fought against the lump that suddenly formed in his throat. 'Anyway, I belong here with you and John, and…'

Much stopped talking as he and Will froze;

they could just hear the faint sound of people approaching.

They were about to take cover when Much smiled happily. 'Look, it's Robin and the others!'

'*Way* too late to help,' Will tutted, but with good humour.

'I bet they waited to stop that tax-gatherer man before coming to see if we needed them.'

'I'm sure they did. Hopefully that Welsh devil is explaining to De Rainault right now why he ain't got no tax money again. Ha. Third time unlucky.'

'That's something we can all celebrate around the camp's fire tonight, then.'

'Too right, Much. With the rest of my brother's ale!'

'That'd be great, Will! Providing you ain't drunk it all!

Also from Chinbeard and Oak Tree Books

You may also enjoy...

www.ingramcontent.com/pod-product-compliance
Lightning Source LLC
Chambersburg PA
CBHW011515170626
46810CB00009B/3375